She'd just have ~~to prove to all~~ of them that she could do it.

"Training to be a jockey is really hard work."

Melanie frowned. "And you don't think I can work hard?"

Christina shrugged. "Well, it's not like you've ever stuck with anything too seriously for too long. Remember at Camp Saddlebrook when everyone else was slaving away, trying to earn points, and you—"

"Camp was different," Melanie cut in. She couldn't believe what her cousin was saying. Of all people, Christina should understand. She sounded just like Kevin. "That wasn't as important."

"Maybe to you," Christina countered. "But to some of the others, like Eliza, who wanted to be a junior instructor, it was."

Perfection swung sideways, and Melanie's fingers tightened on the lead rope. "Well, this is just as important to me," she said, her cheeks flushing with anger.

Tears filled Melanie's eyes. She reined Pirate away from the fence. Why didn't anyone believe her? She'd just have to prove to all of them that she could do it.

Collect all the books in the
THOROUGHBRED series

THOROUGHBRED Super Editions

ASHLEIGH'S Thoroughbred Collection

* coming soon

THOROUGHBRED

DEAD HEAT

CREATED BY
JOANNA CAMPBELL

WRITTEN BY
ALICE LEONHARDT

HarperEntertainment
A Division of HarperCollins*Publishers*

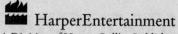

HarperEntertainment

A Division of HarperCollins*Publishers*
10 East 53rd Street, New York, NY 10022-5299

 Produced by 17th Street Productions, a division
of Daniel Weiss Associates, Inc.

HarperCollins books are available at special quantity discounts for bulk
purchases for sales promotions, premiums, or fund-raising.
For information, please call or write:
Special Markets Department, HarperCollins Publishers,
10 East 53rd Street, New York, NY 10022-5299.
Telephone: (212) 207-7528. Fax: (212) 207-7222.

ISBN 0-06-106564-1

HarperCollins®, 🎬®, and HarperEntertainment™
are trademarks of HarperCollins Publishers Inc.

Cover art © 1999 by Daniel Weiss Associates, Inc.

First printing: July 1999

Printed in the United States of America

Visit HarperEntertainment on the World Wide Web at
http://www.harpercollins.com

❖ 10 9 8 7 6 5 4 3 2 1

1

THE WIND BUFFETED MELANIE GRAHAM'S CHEEKS AS PRIDE'S Perfection thundered past the finish line. Melanie stood in her stirrups and raised both arms over her head in victory, her heart bursting with excitement. She had done it! She'd won the Kentucky Derby!

The crowd cheered and Melanie waved to the audience in the grandstand as Perfection danced proudly to the winner's circle. An official draped the blanket of roses around Perfection's neck while photographers and reporters clustered around them, snapping pictures, shouting questions.

"Melanie? Can you answer the question, please?"

Startled out of her fantasy, Melanie Graham jerked upright. At the front of the classroom, Ms. Hanlon, her eighth-grade English teacher, was staring expectantly at her.

"Uh . . ." Melanie hadn't heard Miss Hanlon's question. How was she supposed to know the answer?

Nervously Melanie tugged on a wisp of her short blond hair. Her gaze shifted to her friend Dylan Becker, who sat at the desk across the aisle from her. Lowering his hand, he pointed to the blackboard where Miss Hanlon had written, THE HORSE RACED ACROSS THE FIELD. IT JUMPED THE FENCE.

"Um, you could add, 'And they won the steeplechase'?" Melanie guessed.

When the other students in the classroom cracked up, Melanie wondered what was so funny.

"That's not exactly what I was looking for," Miss Hanlon said. "Katie? Can you tell me what to do?"

"You could combine them using a conjunction," Katie Garrity, another of Melanie's friends, replied.

"That's correct. What conjunction could you use?"

Several hands went up. Melanie rolled her eyes. Who cared about conjunctions? There were too many other things to think about. Like riding. That afternoon Naomi Traeger, an apprentice jockey and exercise rider at Whitebrook Farm, was helping Melanie practice her racing position. She couldn't wait.

"For homework, combine the sentences on page eighty-four in your English book," Ms. Hanlon told the class just as the bell rang. Melanie hastily filled in her assignment book, then stuck it in her backpack. English was the last period of the day. She was free!

Jumping up from her seat, she headed for the door.

"Melanie!" Ms. Hanlon's stern voice stopped her in her tracks.

Melanie grimaced. "Yes?" She turned around just as Dylan went past. "Sounds like trouble," he said under his breath.

Melanie shrugged. She was used to trouble. Last year, when she'd lived in New York City, she'd spent as much time in the principal's office as she had in the classroom.

"I need to speak with you a minute," Ms. Hanlon said. When Melanie walked over, Ms. Hanlon tapped her open grade book. "I'm concerned about the assignments you're missing."

"I'm sorry, Ms. Hanlon," Melanie said, laying the sincerity on thick. "I guess I'm having trouble adjusting to the new school. It's a lot different here than in New York."

The teacher nodded. "I understand, but I do expect you to catch up. Let me know if there's anything I can do."

How about not assigning so much homework? Melanie wanted to say. Instead, she smiled sweetly. "I will. Thanks for being concerned, and I'll have the missing work finished by next week."

"Good. I'll be expecting it."

Slinging her backpack over her shoulder, Melanie hurried out the door and down the busy hall of Henry Clay Middle School. Her cousin, Christina Reese, was waiting by Melanie's locker.

At the beginning of the summer, Melanie had moved in with Christina and her family at Whitebrook, a Thoroughbred breeding and training farm in Kentucky. She and Christina had had their share of problems, but usually they got along well.

"You'd better hurry or we'll miss the bus," Christina said. "I want to get home and ride Sterling. Sam's giving me—"

"I want to get home, too," Melanie interrupted. "In fact, I've wanted to get home since I left this morning. I don't know why I bother with school. It's soooo boring." Opening her locker, she threw her backpack inside.

Christina raised her eyebrows in surprise. "Don't you have any homework?"

"Nah." Melanie tried to shut the locker door, but the bottom of the backpack stuck out. Impatiently she pushed and shoved, finally cramming it inside.

"Hey, Chris, are you riding at Whisperwood this afternoon?" Dylan called as he came down the hall with a stream of students.

"Yes," Christina said when Dylan joined them. "I'm hacking Sterling over for a five o'clock lesson."

"Do you think Sam would take on one more student?" he asked. Samantha Nelson and her husband, Tor, old friends of Christina's family, had recently moved back to Kentucky from Ireland to set up their own eventing stable, Whisperwood Farm.

Christina shrugged. "Why don't you come over this afternoon and ask her?"

"I'll do that."

Slamming the locker door, Melanie turned and scanned the crowd of students.

"If you're looking for Kevin, he's got basketball tryouts," Dylan reminded her.

Kevin McLean was Melanie's boyfriend, sort of. At least he was always around. He lived at Whitebrook, too, since his father, Ian McLean, was the farm's head trainer. Kevin loved horses just as much as Melanie did, and when school sports didn't cut into his time, he worked with the weanlings for Mike Reese, Christina's father. Mike owned Whitebrook Farm with Ashleigh Griffin, Christina's mom.

Melanie was disappointed. "I was hoping he'd be around this afternoon," she said.

Christina pushed open the exit doors. "What's going on this afternoon?" she asked.

"Naomi's helping me practice riding with shorter stirrups. If I want to ride in the Kentucky Derby one day, I'd better concentrate on learning to be a jockey."

Dylan laughed. "The Kentucky Derby? No offense, but I wouldn't get my hopes up too high, Mel."

"Hey, if Christina can dream about eventing in the Olympics, I can dream about winning the Kentucky Derby." Melanie punched him playfully on the arm. "And you can dream about a multimillion-dollar contract with the Atlanta Braves," she teased.

"Maybe I'll be competing against you instead," Dylan joked back.

Christina and Dylan were both good riders, and they liked each other, too. *At least they used to like each other,* Melanie thought. Ever since Parker Townsend had come home to live with his family nearby, Christina had been intrigued by the ninth grader. Christina still hadn't made up her mind which boy she liked better.

"Let's face it. We're all destined to be great at something someday," Melanie said dramatically.

Linking arms with her two friends, she propelled them down the sidewalk to the waiting bus. She couldn't wait to get to Whitebrook. For the first time in her life, Melanie was really good at something—riding racehorses. Everyone said she was the perfect size. Everyone said she had the natural talent.

Melanie loved it more than anything, and she was determined to be the best.

"Melanie Graham is taking Perfection to the outside for a clear run," Naomi Traeger said in the singsong voice of an announcer. "Down the stretch they come, and Perfection and Flame are tied. It looks like it's going to be a dead heat. But wait, Graham and Perfection are pulling ahead. It's Perfection by a nose!"

Exhausted, Melanie plopped back into the tiny racing saddle. Her arms ached; her legs trembled.

Naomi clapped her on the back. "You made it. One minute in the racing position without losing your balance." Naomi was seventeen and had been exercising racehorses at Whitebrook for several years. She was also an apprentice jockey, or "bug rider," as they called it around the track. The week before, she'd won her first race on Leap of Faith, a Whitebrook filly. To become a fully licensed jockey, she had to have thirty-five wins.

"Only one minute!" Melanie grumbled. "It felt like ten. And it wasn't a real race. Or a real horse, for that matter," she added with a laugh.

The two girls had dragged three hay bales behind the barn, stacked them on top of each other, then stuck a tiny racing saddle on the pile. Naomi had also managed to attach reins to the top bale so Melanie would have something to hold on to.

For the past month Melanie had been exercising several of Whitebrook's racehorses. Even after a few rocky rides and a fall off Heart of Stone, she still loved it. But exercise riders rode in a bigger saddle with longer stirrup leathers. A jockey's saddle was tiny and the stirrups were so short, the rider was perched precariously on top of the horse. Naomi had warned her that it wasn't going to be easy.

"You're going to have to work on upper-body and leg strength." Naomi squeezed Melanie's arm muscle.

"You mean lift weights?" Melanie asked.

Naomi nodded. "I work out every day."

"Wow. I had no idea. What about my weight?"

"You need to stay below one hundred and ten."

"I'm way below that."

"Now. But you're only thirteen," Naomi pointed

out. "The older you get, the more weight you'll put on. What you're really going to have to work on is balance—that's the hardest to master and the most important."

"How do I do that?"

"Ride, ride, ride," Naomi said, laughing. "Then ride some more."

Melanie grinned. "No problem."

Naomi checked her watch. "I've gotta go. Why don't you practice on Old Hay Bales here a while longer?"

Melanie nodded. Gathering her reins, she put her toes in her stirrups and shifted her body forward. Immediately she lost her balance. Frowning, she tried again, managing to stay up for a couple of seconds before falling forward. With a sigh of dismay, she sat back.

This isn't easy, Melanie thought. The next time she stood up in the stirrups, she stayed up.

One day I'll be racing a real horse, Melanie told herself as she pumped her arms, urging on Old Hay Bales. *One day I'll ride in the Kentucky Derby, and being in the winner's circle won't be just a dream.*

2

"WHOA! RUNAWAY HAY BALES!" KEVIN MCLEAN EXCLAIMED when he came around the corner of the barn.

Melanie laughed. "No way. I've got them under control," she said, pulling hard on the reins. The bales began to tip.

"Oh, no," Melanie cried as she tipped with them. Before she could catch herself, the bales fell sideways, and she tumbled to the grass beside them.

Kevin hurried over. His auburn hair was damp; his blue eyes twinkled. Holding out his hand, he offered to help her up. Ignoring him, Melanie jumped to her feet.

"I'm okay," she said quickly.

Kevin bent over and picked up a bale. "You'd better get right back on and show this wild horse who's boss," he joked as he swung it on top of one of the others.

9

"Very funny," Melanie retorted with a laugh. "Are basketball tryouts over?"

"Yeah."

"And?"

"I won't know until tomorrow."

"You know you made the team. Christina says you're the best forward Henry Clay's got. You're the fastest, anyway. Your team was almost unbeatable last season."

Kevin shrugged. "Only this season I'm trying out for the high-school junior varsity team," he said.

"An eighth grader can do that?" Melanie asked.

"Yup. So did you win the Derby?" he asked, nodding toward the hay bales.

"No." Melanie sighed. "When I watched Naomi race Faith and win, it looked so easy. It's not."

"It's all balance," Kevin stated authoritatively. Like Melanie, Kevin had just started exercising racehorses.

"Like you know?" Melanie teased as she picked up the racing saddle, which had fallen, too. "After one 'race' on Thunder?"

For practice, Melanie, Kevin, and Naomi had run a mock race recently. Naomi on Faith had soundly beaten the other two horses, but it had still been fun.

"I've been around racehorses and jockeys all my life," Kevin reminded her. "That's all my sisters, Cindy and Samantha, ever wanted to do. So I know what it takes—a lot of hard work and practice." Crossing his arms, he eyed her skeptically.

"Why are you looking at me like that?" Melanie asked. "Don't you think I can do it?"

Kevin raised his brows. "I never said that. But now that you mention it, since you've been at Whitebrook you've jumped from one thing to another awfully quickly. First it was lessons on Trib. Then dressage, Camp Saddlebrook, and eventing. Then ponying on Pirate . . ."

Melanie bristled. "That's because it took me a while to decide what I wanted to do. Then I discovered racing."

Kevin raised one hand. "I believe you. Don't bite my head off."

"Sorry. But you sounded like my father," Melanie said. "I think the only reason he gave me permission to exercise the Thoroughbreds was because he figured I wouldn't stick with it."

When Kevin didn't say anything, Melanie looked sideways at him. Did Kevin think the same thing?

Oh, who cares what he thinks, Melanie decided. She knew she was serious about being a jockey, and that's what was important.

Clutching the saddle to her chest, she headed around the side of the training barn. The late afternoon sun was bright, casting a glow over Whitebrook's barns and pastures. The leaves had changed colors, and frost covered the ground every morning. Except for the broodmares and the weaned foals, all the horses were in the barn for the night.

"So what about you? Do you ever think about racing?" Melanie asked Kevin.

"Sometimes. But I figure I'll probably get too big to be a jockey."

She stopped in front of the barn's double doors. "Too bad. You're competitive enough."

Kevin grinned. "Yeah, I know. In fact, I have a secret to tell you. I would have been really mad if you and Stone had beaten me and old Thunder in that silly race."

Melanie was about to tease Kevin back when she noticed his serious expression. "You're not joking, are you?"

"Nope." He rocked back on his heels. "I hate to lose." He paused, as if he was going to add something, but didn't go on.

"Especially to a girl," Melanie added, starting to get angry. "Is that what you were going to say?"

"No. I hate to lose, period." He grinned again, and for a second Melanie wondered if he was joking. But then she thought about his baseball and soccer teams. Not only was Kevin one of the best players, but his teams usually won.

"And all this time I thought you were a nice guy," Melanie muttered.

"I am." Reaching down, he plucked the saddle from her arms. "I'm a nice guy who likes to win." He flashed her another grin, then strode down the aisle to the tack room. Melanie shook her head. She didn't have time to

12

wonder about Kevin and his attitude. She needed to hose down Perfection's leg.

Several weeks earlier the two-year-old had stumbled and fallen during a workout, tossing Melanie and pulling a muscle in his right foreleg. The vet had said the leg could take months to heal. Melanie had felt terrible, even though the fall hadn't been her fault. Now, part of his daily care was up to her. The hosing and walking were boring, but it helped her get to know the rambunctious colt better, and she felt less guilty knowing she was helping the colt's leg to heal.

"Hey, big guy," Melanie said when she came up to his stall door. Startled, he threw up his head, a hunk of hay hanging from his mouth. Pride's Perfection was a deep copper color, and just as big and handsome as his father, Pride's Chance. Melanie knew that her aunt and uncle had big plans for the two-year-old once his pulled muscle had completely healed.

Opening the stall door, Melanie went in. "How's your leg today?" she asked as she bent over and ran her hand down it. The leg felt cool and there was no swelling, both good signs.

"Why don't you use Pirate to pony him?" a voice suggested.

Melanie looked up to see Ian, Kevin's dad, standing in the doorway of the stall. He had Kevin's reddish hair, though his was now laced with gray.

"He needs more exercise than just hand walking," Ian went on. "I don't want to turn him out yet because he might get too full of himself and pull that muscle all over again."

"Do you think I can hold him?" Melanie asked.

Ian grinned. "Pirate will know what to do with him."

Pirate's Treasure was a promising racehorse that had gone blind unexpectedly. He'd grown depressed until Melanie had convinced everybody that he missed the track. Ian had worked with Melanie, teaching her and Pirate how to pony the young Thoroughbreds, leading them to and from the track. Pirate was a good teacher, too. If Ian turned Pirate out with a bratty young horse, Pirate would quickly teach the younger animal some manners with a few well-placed nips.

"Okay," Melanie agreed. She liked the idea since it would be easier than walking him. "I'll groom Pirate and tack him up. He'll be happy to do some work."

As if Pirate had heard his name, he whinnied from the stall next door.

"Tell me when you're ready and I'll bring Perfection out to you," Ian said before leaving.

"Sure." Melanie patted Perfection, then left him to finish eating his hay. When she walked over to Pirate's stall, he greeted her with a low nicker. "I think you must smell me coming," she said. "Or could it be the carrot in my pocket?"

Opening the stall door, she held out the treat. He snorted at her shirt, then lowered his head and lipped it carefully from her palm. While he crunched happily, she led him by the halter into the aisle and hooked him to the crossties.

Pirate was pure black, and since Melanie had been caring for him, his coat shone like polished ebony. As she curried him, she ran her fingers along the scar on his chest. Before they'd discovered he was going blind, Pirate had crashed through the inside railing on the training track, injuring himself.

"Just a quick brushing today," Melanie told him as she tacked him up with a regular saddle. The late afternoon air was brisk, and she would need a deep seat in order to hold Perfection back.

When Pirate was ready, Melanie zipped on her chaps and snapped on her helmet. Then she looked around for Ian. He was standing in front of the double doors, talking to Kevin. They both had serious expressions on their faces, and Kevin was staring at his feet.

"If I make the team, we'll have practice every afternoon Monday through Thursday," Melanie heard Kevin tell his dad.

"That's going to cut into your time at the farm," Ian said. "You took on the job of working with the yearlings, remember? Mike's counting on you."

"Don't worry, I'll make it up on the weekends," Kevin said. "Mike said I could keep breezing T-Bone every morning, too. After all, I'm going to need the money if I want to go to that basketball clinic." His tone changed and he suddenly sounded angry. "I know you don't think the clinic's important, Dad, but I—" Just then he noticed Melanie standing in the aisle and he stopped talking.

Melanie flushed. She'd never heard Kevin get mad at his dad before. *So that's why he was suddenly so interested in exercising the racehorses,* Melanie thought. Melanie had flattered herself that Kevin was just coming up with ways to spend more time with her, but it sounded more as though Kevin just wanted to make some extra money.

"I'm ready," Melanie called to Ian. Kevin turned and strode away from the barn. When he was gone, she led Pirate over to the mounting block. He stood patiently until she was in the saddle. Only then did he show his eagerness.

Several minutes later Ian led Perfection across the grassy area between the three barns. Head high, the colt pranced at the end of the lead line, his coat gleaming in the evening sun. "I looped the chain over his nose just in case," Ian said. "You'll need to hold him close and keep him at a walk."

"Where should I take him?" Melanie asked. "I'm not going near the track. He'll think he's racing."

"Walk around the back pasture. I'll shut the gate. That way if he does break free, he won't get in too much trouble."

Melanie reached for the lead line. "Don't worry, Pirate and I won't let him get away with anything. Right, boy?"

Just then Perfection danced sideways, bumping his hindquarters into Pirate's rump. The black horse

16

pinned his ears threateningly. Melanie laughed when Perfection immediately scooted over. "You tell him who's boss, Pirate."

Holding the colt's head close to her thigh, Melanie rode toward the pasture. She neck-reined Pirate with the other hand, but mostly he responded to a light cue from her leg or shift of her weight. Because he was blind, he'd had to learn to trust her signals to guide him.

Halfway to the pasture, Perfection snorted at a shadow and tried to run backward. Pirate backed up, too, so Melanie could keep a firm grip on the colt's head. Annoyed, Perfection tried to rear, but Pirate stepped into him, forcing the colt down. Finally realizing he wasn't going to get away with any foolishness, Perfection settled into a walk.

Melanie breathed a sigh of relief. "Good job, buddy," she praised Pirate as they strode through the gate into the pasture.

For the next twenty minutes she worked the two horses up and down the hills. When Perfection was walking quietly, Melanie's mind started to wander.

She imagined she was mounted on Perfection and a pony rider was on Pirate as they headed for the race-track. "Won't be long," she said, reaching over to stroke his neck.

Suddenly Perfection slammed to a halt, surprising Pirate, who stopped dead, too. Melanie lurched forward, grabbing a handful of mane to keep from falling off.

"What was that for?" Melanie scolded Pirate, angry

at herself for not paying attention. For a second the two horses stood frozen as they stared toward the woods. Melanie wondered what they were looking at. Just then her cousin, Christina, rode out of the woods astride her gray mare, Sterling Dream. Christina waved as she walked her mare down the fence line between the pastures.

"Hello!" Melanie called. "It's only Sterling, you goose," she told Perfection, who continued to stare, his brown eyes huge. "Come on. Let's go say hi."

She steered Pirate over to the fence. Sterling stopped and snorted as they approached. The usually sleek hair on her dappled neck was dull and rough with dried sweat. "How was your lesson?"

"Hard, but great," Christina said. "Samantha worked us over a couple of really tough courses."

"Who else was there?"

"Dylan came over, and he and Parker watched."

Melanie felt a pang of jealousy. She had always enjoyed jumping lessons with all her friends, but now Dylan and Christina had moved beyond her in eventing, and jumping around and around a course in a ring under the careful instruction of their old teacher, Mona Gardener, wasn't quite her thing anymore, either.

"Parker can't wait to start working Foxy again," Christina continued. "He gets his cast off in a couple of weeks." Parker had fallen in an event recently, breaking his arm.

"Did Dylan ask Sam about taking lessons with her?"

18

Christina nodded. "She said she'd love to have him."

"What do you think about that?" Melanie's eyes twinkled. "Dylan and Parker both at Whisperwood."

Christina laughed. "I guess I can handle it." She pointed to Perfection. "Hey, how's his leg?"

"The swelling's down and it feels cool. Ian said he needs to start building his muscles back up. That's why I'm ponying him," Melanie answered.

"He looks good. Do you think my mom and dad will let you ride him again?" Christina asked.

"I hope so. I'd love to be the one to get him ready for his first big race. I couldn't be his jockey, though. Yet," Melanie added emphatically. "But the minute I turn sixteen I'm going to become an apprentice jockey."

Christina cocked one brow. "You think you'll stick with it that long?"

"What do you mean?" Melanie asked.

"Training to be a jockey is really hard work."

Melanie frowned. "And you don't think I can work hard?"

Christina shrugged. "Well, it's not like you've ever stuck with anything too seriously for too long. Remember at Camp Saddlebrook when everyone else was slaving away, trying to earn points, and you—"

"Camp was different," Melanie cut in. She couldn't believe what her cousin was saying. Of all people, Christina should understand. She sounded just like Kevin. "That wasn't as important."

"Maybe to you," Christina countered. "But to some of the others, like Eliza, who wanted to be a junior instructor, it was."

Perfection swung sideways, and Melanie's fingers tightened on the lead rope. "Well, this is just as important to me," she said, her cheeks flushing with anger.

Tears filled Melanie's eyes. She reined Pirate away from the fence. Why didn't anyone believe her? She'd just have to prove to all of them that she could do it.

3

"MELANIE, WAIT!" CHRISTINA CALLED.

Melanie kept Pirate walking forward. She heard the thud of hooves on the grass, and then Christina was beside her on the other side of the fence.

"You misunderstood me," Christina explained. "I'm glad to see you're finally serious about something."

"You mean it?" Melanie asked, halting Pirate and Perfection and avoiding her cousin's eyes.

"Of course I mean it, Mel," Christina insisted.

"Oh. I guess I kind of overreacted. Sorry, Chris, but no one seems to understand how serious I am about becoming a jockey."

"I do. You sound like me when I tell my mother how I'm going to be on the next winning Olympic eventing team." Christina laced her fingers through Sterling's mane.

"And you will," Melanie said. "Especially with Samantha as your new instructor."

"Samantha is a cool teacher," Christina agreed. "I wish you would take a lesson with us sometime."

"Over those big jumps?" Melanie shook her head. "No way. Besides, Samantha's promised to help me on the track, too. That's what's so cool about her—she knows eventing, breeding, training, racing. She can do it all. "

Christina cocked her head. "Yeah. Sam told me she loved riding racehorses, but she never regretted being too big to be a jockey because she loved eventing just as much." Christina shrugged and patted Sterling, who began to paw the grass impatiently. "Anyway, I'd better get her washed off."

Melanie hadn't realized how dark it was growing. She shivered in the cool air. As she turned Pirate and Perfection toward the gate, she saw Ian waiting at the bottom of the pasture. Both horses quickened their paces, eager to get back to the barn.

"How'd he do?" Ian asked when they reached the gate. Bending down, he quickly ran his hands over Perfection's leg. "No puffiness. And it's still cool." He took the lead line from Melanie. "If everything goes well, we can start light workouts next week."

"Do you think I'll be able to ride him?" Melanie asked.

"That's up to Ashleigh and Mike."

At least he didn't say no, Melanie thought as she followed Ian into the barn. She dismounted in the aisle, slipped off Pirate's bridle, put on his halter, and hooked him in the crossties. Ian had Perfection in another set of crossties and was rubbing his front legs with liniment.

Melanie checked her watch. It was five-thirty. Even though it was dark, there was still time to ride before dinner. Naomi had said the best practice was to ride, ride, ride. Melanie knew it was too late to take out one of the racehorses, but there was no reason she couldn't saddle up Trib.

After grooming Pirate and putting him away, she headed for the mare and foal barn, where Kevin's horse, Jasper, Christina's pony, Trib (short for Tribulation), and Sterling were kept.

Christina was walking Sterling around the grassy courtyard. The mare wore a blue and white cooler to keep her from getting chilled while she dried.

"Where are you headed?" Christina asked as she stopped Sterling and checked under the lightweight blanket to see if she was cooled down.

"To see Trib," Melanie said. "Hey, pretty girl." She ran her hand along Sterling's dark gray neck. The mare was a gorgeous Thoroughbred who'd hated the racetrack. Christina was retraining her for eventing. "I want to see how Pride's Heart is doing, too."

"She's growing like a weed," Christina said. "Too bad she's a fall foal."

All Thoroughbreds turned a year old on January 1. It was to their advantage to be born after New Year's

Day so they'd have a full two years of growth before they began racing. Heart had been born that fall, so when the filly turned officially two, she'd really be just over a year old.

"Well, I'm sure they'll start her only when she's ready, and if she grows as big and strong as her brother, Perfection, it won't matter anyway," Melanie said before continuing into the barn.

As she walked down the aisle, she stopped to say hi to the mares that still had foals by their sides. By now, most of the foals had been weaned and were turned out together in one of the pastures.

"Hey, Momma," Melanie crooned when she opened the door to Perfect Heart's stall. Busy with her hay, the mare ignored her. Melanie waited patiently and soon a gawky, fuzzy-faced foal with a heart-shaped star on her forehead peeked around her mother, then ambled over.

"Hi, cutie pie," Melanie crooned. She scratched the foal on the neck. "I wonder if your brother, Perfection, was this friendly when he was your age, or if he was already a brat."

As if to prove she was just as feisty, the foal ducked her head and bucked playfully. Losing her balance in the thick straw, she fell against her mother's side. Perfect Heart turned her head to make sure her baby was okay, then went back to eating.

Melanie leaned back against the stall wall and let her thoughts wander as she watched the foal. She could become an apprentice jockey when she was sixteen. By then, Pride's Heart would be a three-year-old. If she was as talented as her brother, the filly might be the horse Melanie rode in her first race.

"Yup, it might be you and me in the winner's circle," Melanie told the long-legged foal. "So we'll both have to work extra hard."

Giving the foal a last scratch, she shut the door and strode down the aisle. Trib was scrounging around in the sawdust for the last pieces of his hay.

Melanie grabbed a grooming box and halter from the tack room. "Hey, chubby," she teased the pinto. Trib had been Christina's show pony until she outgrew him and got Sterling. He was just the right size for Melanie, and—everyone said—just the right temperament. They were both hardheaded and unpredictable.

When Melanie opened the door, Trib laid back his ears. She ignored him. "Hello, piggy," she said cheerfully. "Yes, you ate all your hay. You always act like you're starving to death so that people will throw you more hay. Come here so I can torture you."

She slipped on the halter and gave the pony a quick brushing. He was starting to grow a fuzzy winter coat, and his thick mane stuck up uncontrollably.

While Melanie brushed, she thought up a brilliant plan. She'd shorten the stirrups on her own saddle and trot Trib around the back pasture. That would help develop her balance.

Quickly she tacked Trib up and tugged him out of his stall. The pony was more than reluctant to leave, and

Melanie had to keep clucking until they were outside. When he saw Sterling, Trib raised his head and whinnied excitedly to his barn buddy. Sterling whinnied back.

"Where are you going with Trib?" Christina asked. "Isn't it kind of late?" The lights at the end of the barns were on, but the area beyond was pitch black.

"Naomi told me I've got to strengthen my arms and legs and improve my balance," Melanie said, halting Trib by the mounting block. "And the only way to do that is to ride every chance I get."

"But it's dark," Christina countered.

"I'm only going in the pasture. Trib knows his way around." Melanie shortened the stirrups as much as she could.

"What are you doing now?"

"Riding Trib jockey style."

Christina let out a burst of laughter. "You'd better hang on. Trib's no smooth-moving Thoroughbred."

"Hey, if I can breeze a racehorse, I think I can handle this guy," Melanie insisted.

"If you say so," Christina said in a teasing voice.

Melanie ignored her. Trib was known for bucking and running off, but since she'd ridden him all summer, she'd learned to handle him.

Standing on the mounting block, Melanie vaulted into the saddle. It took a few minutes to get her feet in the stirrups. They weren't as short as the ones on the racing saddle, but they definitely made her sit high on Trib's back.

Christina held a pretend microphone to her mouth. "And here's the mighty Tribulation, heading for the finish line," she announced, sounding like Naomi. "Will he make it before the smell of popcorn wafting from the stands breaks his concentration?"

"Now look who's not being serious," Melanie told her cousin. "Don't worry, I won't be late for dinner."

"It's probably soup and sandwiches, anyway," Christina said. "The vet's coming to check some of the mares in a little while to make sure they're still in foal. You know my mom won't want to miss that."

"Come on, Trib," Melanie said as she steered him away from the mounting block. They made it around the end of the barn, but then the pony stopped dead. "I know, I know. It's dark out there. But we're only going for a short ride. I promise."

Melanie tried to squeeze him forward with her calves, but her legs were bent at such awkward angles, she couldn't reach his sides. She clucked, but he wouldn't budge. "Trib, you are being really stubborn."

So how did the jockeys get the racehorses to go if they couldn't even kick with their heels? Melanie wondered. Then she realized that most racehorses didn't have trouble going forward. They had trouble slowing down.

"Trib, pretend you're Ashleigh's Wonder about to win the Kentucky Derby," she told him. The pony flicked one ear back but didn't move. Then Sterling whinnied from behind him.

Whirling like a top, Trib took off. Melanie was flung sideways, then forward. Wrapping her arms around his neck, she held on while he raced toward Sterling.

Right in front of Christina, Trib put on his pony brakes. Melanie somersaulted over his head and landed with a thud in the grass at her cousin's feet.

"Are you all right?" Christina asked, kneeling beside her.

Melanie groaned. "Ugh. I think every bone in my body is broken."

"I'll get help!" Christina jumped up.

"No, wait!" Melanie groaned again. "Nothing's busted. On me, that is." Sitting up, she aimed a hateful look at Trib, who stood by Sterling's side, happily cropping grass. "But wait until I get hold of—"

"Calm down, Mel." Christina crouched beside her again, a concerned expression on her face. "Are you sure you're all right? That was quite a tumble." Pressing her lips together, she held back a grin.

"Go ahead. Laugh at me," Melanie grumbled as she brushed off the sleeves of her jacket.

"Well, it's not like I didn't warn you."

Slowly Melanie stood up, checking to make sure nothing really was broken. Before Trib could move away, she snatched up the dangling reins. "Don't even think about running off," she warned.

"Are you getting on him again?"

"You bet." Melanie lifted up the saddle flap. "Only this time I'm lengthening the stirrups a little."

Suddenly Christina started laughing, and Melanie couldn't help but grin. "I wish I'd had a video camera," Christina said. "We could have shown it at our next party."

"You mean along with videos of you falling off Sterling, and Parker crashing Foxy into the fence?" Melanie countered.

"Right. Need a leg up?" Christina offered.

"Thanks, but I'll use the mounting block. And Chris, don't tell your mom or Naomi or—"

"How about if I don't tell anyone?" Christina suggested.

"Great idea." After lowering the stirrups several holes, Melanie swung into the saddle. Her heels reached Trib's fat sides. "Okay, Speedy, this time head for the finish line, not home."

Shortening her reins, she steered him around the barn. Her seat felt more secure, and as she trotted Trib up and down the hills, she worked on balance.

When she was finished, her legs were so tired they trembled. Naomi was right. She needed to start working out.

Half an hour later she'd cooled and groomed Trib, had put him away, and was headed to the house. The porch light was on. It was after six-thirty, but since the vet had just arrived, she figured she wasn't late for dinner.

Christina was sitting at the kitchen table, munching an apple and reading a book. Her backpack was propped against the chair and her notebook was open on the table

"Did I miss dinner?" Melanie asked as she washed her hands.

"No. We're suppose to fix grilled cheese sandwiches," Christina said without looking up from her book. "The stuff's on the counter."

"Good. I'm starved." Melanie dried her hands on her pants, then went over to the counter and started slicing cheese.

Christina closed her book. "I'm done with civics. So how did you and Trib do?"

"Terrible. I'm going to have to start working out like Naomi," Melanie answered.

"She works out?" Christina asked.

"Every day. That's what she told me."

"No wonder she's such a strong rider."

"Yeah, and why she's so good, too. Are you ready for a sandwich?" Melanie held up a slice of bread. "Anyway, I need to come up with an exercise program. Want to do it with me?" Melanie asked.

Christina eyed her over the open refrigerator door. "It depends on what's involved," she said warily.

"We could get up early. Jog, do some sit-ups, lift some weights—Kevin has some we could borrow," Melanie suggested.

"But you already get up at six to gallop Stone," Christina argued.

"True. I'll get up half an hour earlier to gallop him,

then wake you up to exercise. What do you think?" she asked.

Christina hesitated, a dubious expression on her face.

"Hey, aren't you the person who wants to make the Olympic team?" Melanie asked.

"But that's years from now," Christina protested as she shut the refrigerator door.

"Right. But we've gotta start training right now if we're really serious about this." Pulling the knife from the butter, Melanie pointed it at her cousin. "After dinner we'll come up with an exercise plan."

"Okay," Christina finally agreed. "I'll try it for a week. But if it gets too crazy, I may quit. Unlike some eighth graders I know, I have a lot of homework every night."

Melanie ignored her. "Great. Tonight we'll decide what exercises we want to do, then we'll start tomorrow morning." Grinning excitedly, she waved her knife in the air. "Stick with me, Christina Reese, and we'll go all the way to the top!"

4

"CHRISTINA, WAKE UP." MELANIE SAT ON THE EDGE OF HER cousin's bed and gave her shoulder a shake. It was Tuesday morning, and Melanie had been up for half an hour. "It's six. Time to exercise."

Christina groaned loudly and rolled on her side. "Go 'way."

Melanie shook her harder. When she didn't budge, Melanie jumped up and flicked on the overhead light.

Christina threw her arm over her eyes. "What did you do that for?"

"Wake up, sleepyhead," Melanie sang. Waving her arms, she hopped in place. She'd changed from her breeches and boots into shorts and a sweatshirt, but the morning air was chilly and she didn't want to stiffen up. "I've already exercised Stone. We had a great ride!" Still her cousin didn't move. Reaching down, Melanie snatched off the covers. "Rise and shine."

"Hey!" Christina struggled to a sitting position, but when she grabbed for the blanket, Melanie pulled it away.

"Oh, all right." With a grumpy expression, Christina climbed out of bed. Melanie handed her shorts and a sweatshirt.

"I'll meet you in the kitchen. Don't fall back asleep. You promised you'd try it for a week. Remember?"

"Yeah, yeah," Christina grumbled as she headed for the bathroom.

Humming cheerfully, Melanie trotted down the steps to the family's big country kitchen. She didn't know why Christina was having such a hard time getting up. Ashleigh and Mike were at the barns supervising workouts by six every morning.

That day Melanie had beaten them. Mike didn't believe in feeding until after workouts, so it hadn't taken her long to groom Stone and ride.

If she continued to get to the barn by five-thirty, she'd have plenty of time to exercise, shower, eat, and get to the bus stop by a quarter to eight.

A few minutes later Christina came downstairs. Melanie handed her a plain toasted English muffin.

Christina wrinkled her nose. "What's this?"

"Breakfast." Melanie took a bite of hers before heading out the door.

Christina took a bite, then pretended to gag. "It tastes like sawdust."

"Wouldn't know. I've never eaten sawdust. But if we're going to be lean and mean, we've got to cut out some of the fat and sugar."

Christina groaned. "You sound like Ms. Waters, my fifth-grade health teacher."

"How about if we jog down the lane to the road and back?" Melanie suggested when they were outside. The sun was just rising, and the grass was dusted with frost.

Christina nodded and broke into a trot. Melanie took off next to her. For a minute they ran in silence. The cold morning air slapped Melanie's cheeks and stung her eyes. When they reached the end of the lane, she was puffing.

"You would have thought all those laps around the track for PE would've conditioned us a little," she said, turning to jog back.

Christina didn't say anything. She had a serious expression on her face. *Good*, Melanie thought. She hoped her cousin would keep going with her every morning.

When they reached the house, Christina flopped on the steps of the front porch. "That was hard work," she gasped. The tip of her nose and tops of her ears were bright red.

"We did about a mile, I think." Melanie jogged in place. "Let's go inside and do sit-ups and push-ups."

They were in the middle of push-ups when Ashleigh stopped in the family room doorway. "Are you girls eating breakfast before school?" she asked, giving them a curious look.

Melanie collapsed facedown on the rug. "I had mine. An apple and an English muffin."

"Can you fix me a couple of pieces of buttered raisin toast, please?" Christina said between breaths. "With cinnamon and sugar."

"She means plain," Melanie corrected. Christina shot her an annoyed look, then gasped, "Twenty!" and dropped onto the rug.

"Are you girls exercising for a special reason?" Ashleigh asked.

Melanie sat up. "Definitely. You'll be proud of us, too, Aunt Ashleigh. We decided that if I'm going to win the Derby and Chris is going to get a gold at the Olympics, we'd better start training now."

"Uh-huh," Ashleigh said. "As long as it doesn't interfere with schoolwork."

Melanie chewed on a fingernail, avoiding her aunt's gaze.

"Don't worry, I studied plenty last night," Christina said. "I have a science test today."

Melanie felt a pang of panic. She and Christina had the same teacher at different times, but Melanie didn't remember anything about a test.

"Good." Ashleigh's stern expression softened. "Not that school ever stopped me from being with Wonder every chance I could get. My parents were always grounding me, trying to get me to concentrate on my grades."

"Here she goes again, off to the past," Christina teased her mother.

Ashleigh laughed. "Raisin toast, plain, coming right up."

When she left, Melanie whispered, "You're having a test?"

Christina nodded. "Chapters three and four."

"That's what I studied for, too," Melanie said quickly. "Maybe we can quiz each other on the bus ride to school."

Christina gave her a curious look. "You didn't even bring home your book, so how could you study?"

"Uh, we had time in class yesterday." Melanie stood up and stretched. "It was a piece of cake." She headed for the stairs before Christina could accuse her of lying. "I'll take my shower and be out by the time you finish breakfast."

Taking the steps in twos, she went upstairs and into her room and fell face first on the unmade bed. Maybe she'd pretend she was sick so she wouldn't have to go to school. Then she could make up the test later.

"Oh, who cares about the test," she muttered as she rolled over and sat up. Did Julie Krone, Jockey of the Year, worry about school? No. And hadn't Aunt Ashleigh just said she hadn't always done so hot in school, either?

If I'm going to be a jockey, I need to keep focusing on the horses, Melanie decided. Besides, it was what she wanted to do. She'd just have to fit schoolwork in as best she could.

● ● ●

Thursday morning, when Melanie's alarm went off, she was in such a deep sleep it took forever before the beeping woke her. Groggily she reached over and pressed down the lever.

Her bedroom was pitch black and cold. Melanie snuggled down under the covers. It was warm and cozy and she was sooo tired. Just a few more minutes . . .

Someone turning on the shower in the bathroom next door woke her. With a start, Melanie bolted upright. Instantly she knew she'd messed up. A glance at the clock confirmed it. It was six. She wouldn't have time to work out.

Throwing on her jeans and a sweatshirt, she raced down to the kitchen, slipped on her paddock boots, and ran to the barn. So what if she skipped her workout that morning? It was no big deal. She'd worked out faithfully for the past two days. Yesterday, she'd even added weights to the routine.

If she hurried, she'd have time to gallop Stone. Then that night she could work out and run after dinner.

It was a foggy morning, and the sun peeping over the hills made the misty air glimmer. The barns and track were bustling with activity. Melanie scanned the track, counting three pairs of horses and riders. She recognized Naomi on Leap of Faith, and Naomi's brother, Nathan, on Shining Moment, but it was so foggy, she couldn't tell who the third rider was.

Walking over to the railing, she waited for the third pair to gallop around the track. The rider rode smoothly;

the horse had a solid, ground-covering stride. When they came around the bend, it hit her who it was—Kevin on Thunder!

They looked great together, Melanie realized. And she must not have been the only one thinking the same thing. Ian and Mike were at the other end of the oval, watching.

A rush of jealousy rose in Melanie's chest. Kevin was so good at everything. He was great at breaking yearlings and starting two-year-olds. She wished he weren't so interested in exercising the racehorses. She was afraid Mike and Ian might give him the best horses.

And that wouldn't be fair, Melanie thought. She was the one who needed the experience if she was going to be a jockey.

Melanie hurried into the training barn. Maureen Mack, Ian's assistant trainer, was already tacking up Heart of Stone, a dark bay. "Hey, Stoney boy," Melanie greeted him, adding a pat on his sleek neck.

"I was wondering if you were going to show up this morning," Maureen said in her no-nonsense voice. "I was about to put Kevin up on him."

"Kevin?"

"Sure. Why not?"

"But he doesn't have any experience."

Maureen gave her a funny look.

"All right, I don't have much experience, either," Melanie admitted. "But the only horse Kevin's galloped is old T-Bone."

Maureen snorted as she tightened Stone's girth. "Kevin rode before he could walk. He's probably ridden more horses than anyone on the farm. I can't count how many babies he's started. Besides, he's a natural. He can learn in a week what other riders have to really work for."

You mean riders like me? Melanie wanted to snap. Then she remembered how Ashleigh and Mike had praised her for her natural talent. She'd just have to prove they were right.

She'd be the first one in the training barn every morning. Her horse would shine the brightest and have the best workout. She'd listen, watch, and learn from everyone else on the farm. Then she'd have no reason to be jealous of Kevin McLean.

Rushing into the tack room, she found her chaps and helmet. After putting on her gear, she marched from the barn with a determined jut to her chin.

Stone stood next to Maureen, his ears pricked as he watched a tractor with a manure spreader chug up the drive. He was a talented three-year-old who ran hot and cold. Some days he gave it his all. Some days he dawdled. Because he'd been so slow to mature, Mike hadn't put him in a race yet.

Melanie took the reins from Maureen. "All right, big guy," she told him, looking him in the eye. "Let's have a great workout this morning."

Maureen gave her a leg up, then walked with her to the training oval. The other three riders had finished and were walking their horses. All eyes would be on Melanie.

"What do you want me to do with him this morning?" Melanie asked Maureen.

"You've been galloping him easy all week," Maureen said. "Today Ian wants you to breeze him. Show him the whip if you need to. Mike's going to clock him, see if he's ready to race."

Melanie's heart skipped a beat. "You're serious?"

"Of course. You've been working him for a few weeks now and he's in prime condition. He's as ready as he'll ever be. Ian and Mike just need to figure out what kind of race would be best for him."

"Wow." Melanie let out her breath. All thoughts about Kevin disappeared. Mike, Ian, Maureen—all three felt she was good enough to show them what Stone could do.

She wouldn't let them down.

Melanie listened intently as Maureen gave her directions. Then she said, "One of the things I have trouble with is controlling him when he's going full tilt. Any suggestions?"

Maureen nodded. "One of the most important things a good jockey does is rate her mount. An out-of-control racehorse is dangerous. You have to learn to anticipate what your horse is going to do before he gets away from you. Otherwise you're too late and you end up fighting with him instead of using that power to win."

Melanie furrowed her brow, taking in every word. She stroked Stone's neck. He stood quietly, watching the other horses. "It's something you learn, Melanie, the more you ride."

"It makes sense." She thought back to Trib, how she'd quickly learned that when he humped his back, he was ready to buck. If she pulled his head up and made him move forward, she could prevent it. "Thanks, Maureen. After I ride, will you tell me what I'm doing right and wrong?"

"Sure thing," Maureen promised.

Just then Melanie saw Samantha drive up and park. She got out of her pickup, waved to Melanie and Maureen, then went over to join Ian. Kevin had halted Thunder by the rail, and the three started discussing something.

Melanie's palms started to sweat. Now everyone was here. They'd all be watching. She gulped, then squeezed her heels into Stone's sides and steered him through the gap in the railing. She had to put them out of her mind. She had to focus on Stone and his workout.

"Okay, Stoney. Let's show them what you can do." Heart thumping, Melanie trotted along the outside rail, the wrong way around the track, warming him up. For a second she closed her eyes, blocking out everything but Stone. How was he feeling? His long stride was strong but controlled. Was he feeling lazy? Not quite ready to give it his all this morning?

Opening her eyes, she gauged the set of his head

41

and ears. His jaw was relaxed, his ears at half-mast, his neck long. Melanie put all the signs together. Stone was cold today. To get him to give his all, she was going to have to push him.

Halfway around, she began to work on waking him up. She posted more aggressively, squeezed him with her heels, and urged him with her voice. "Come on, Stone. We can do it."

She wiggled her fingers on the reins until he tucked his head. Slowly she felt his stride lengthen as the power seemed to surge from his head to his hindquarters.

Yes! Melanie forgot about everything but communicating with the horse beneath her. Before she knew it, they were at the half-mile pole.

She slowed him to a walk and turned him toward the inside rail of the oval. Arching his neck, he danced in place. He bobbed his head and pulled on the reins, but his ears flicked back and forth, and she knew he was listening to her, waiting for her signal.

Melanie felt the adrenaline race through her own body. When Mike signaled them to go, she balanced forward, her weight in her heels, turned him toward the wire, and hollered, "Go!"

Leaping in the air, Stone charged down the track. For just a second Melanie bobbled backward. Then she grabbed a hunk of mane, leaned forward, and regained her balance. She began to pump with her arms and her body, feeling the power as Stone pounded around the bend. When she felt him start to swing wide, she used her left rein to ease him back to the rail.

At the half-mile pole she felt him slow. Was he tired? No, she decided. She could still feel his muscles coiled beneath her, and his neck was barely lathered. In typical Stone fashion, he was just losing interest.

"Go, Stoney!" she cried, driving him on with her voice and body. She could feel him accelerate in response.

Fast as the wind they raced toward the wire—past Samantha and the others, past Maureen, who stood by the gap, and past the finish line, so fast that Melanie knew it was Stone's best time ever.

5

MELANIE WANTED TO PUNCH THE AIR AND SHOUT OUT LOUD. Instead she sat back and, with light pulls on the reins, slowed Stone to a trot.

"Good boy!" Melanie crooned. Leaning forward, she scratched his withers. Her legs were shaking, and her arms felt like noodles.

Melanie turned Stone to the outside railing, and he jigged excitedly back up the track. Her lips were chapped by the wind and her mouth was dry, but she couldn't stop grinning. When she jogged past the gap, Maureen gave her a thumbs-up sign. "Good job!" she said.

Up ahead, Ian waved her over. Samantha was smiling. Mike was holding a stopwatch in the air. "A black-letter workout!" he called.

A black letter workout meant the best workout time

for a specific distance on a given day. If this had been a pre-race work at a racetrack, the time would have been printed in the *Daily Racing Form.*

Melanie's heart flip-flopped. That meant she was right. Stone had run his best time ever—and she wasn't even a real jockey yet.

"Tomorrow we'll put Naomi on him," Mike was saying when Melanie halted, "and see how he goes. We can enter him next weekend."

"We ought to enter him this weekend," Ian countered. "It's not too late. The first race on Saturday at Keeneland is a maiden race. He's ready now."

Mike looked up. "Melanie? You think he's ready?"

She nodded eagerly. "Yes. He ... feels ... great." Her words came out in gasps. She hadn't realized how breathless she was from the race, the excitement, and the fact they were actually asking for her opinion.

"Way to go, Melanie," Samantha praised. "You've come a long way in a short time."

"I've worked hard, and everybody's been so much help." She directed her smile to Samantha. Then she patted Stone's lathered neck. "And this big guy seems to finally understand what racing is all about." She glanced around, noticing that Kevin wasn't there. He must have taken Thunder back to the barn. Had he seen their workout?

"The trick is getting the right race for Stone," Mike told Ian. "He starts slow, then heats up."

"But you don't want to put him in too long a race, or

he'll lose focus," Melanie chimed in, surprising herself. Stone had plenty of power; he just needed to be reminded what he was doing. "Naomi will have to work hard to keep his mind on racing—and winning."

"Good advice," Mike told her.

"Well, I'd better get him cooled off," Melanie said almost reluctantly. She didn't want the morning and the good feeling to end.

"And don't be late for the bus," Mike added.

The bus! Melanie had forgotten all about school. She wanted to spend all day at Whitebrook. This was where the excitement was. This was where she belonged, not some stuffy old classroom.

When she walked Stone back to the barn, she saw Kevin washing off Thunder. "Good ride," he congratulated her.

"You too. Old T-Bone is actually starting to look like a racehorse."

"Yeah, and Mike's really surprised. He figured he was finished after his last layup. I think he's got another season in him before he retires."

Melanie halted Stone and dismounted. "They may put Stone in a race this Saturday." Suddenly it dawned on her that Saturday was only two days away.

"Good. It's about time he paid his way. Three years of eating and training is expensive."

Stone lowered his head, and Melanie ruffled his forelock. "You can't think of everything in terms of money, you know. He's just a late bloomer."

"And Ashleigh and Mike are softies. Look how they've kept Pirate around. He certainly doesn't earn his keep."

Melanie plopped her hands on her hips. "He does, too. Besides, when did you get so hardhearted? I thought you loved horses."

Using a scraper, Kevin whisked the excess water off Thunder's back. "I do. I also know how much money one horse costs to buy, feed, and train." His tone turned angry.

"That's true, but the horses earn it back racing."

Kevin stopped in midscrape. "Not always," he said flatly. "You can also pour lots of money into a horse that never wins and go completely broke. I've seen it happen." Dropping the scraper in the bucket, he led Thunder away.

Melanie stared after him. What had that been all about? She wanted to ask before he went into the barn, but she knew she had to hurry or she'd never have time for a shower before the bus arrived. One thing was for certain, though, something strange was going on.

Melanie was almost to the end of the drive when the bus pulled up. "Hurry," Christina hollered before climbing the steps.

Melanie sprinted the last ten yards. "Thanks for waiting," she gasped to the bus driver as she leaped up the steps after her cousin. The bus was crowded. Kevin had already boarded and was sitting next to Dylan. Katie Garrity and Cassidy Smith, a ninth-grader who kept her two horses at Mona's, sat in front of them. Since there were no other seats around their friends, Christina and Melanie sat toward the front.

Not that she'd have time to talk to Kevin anyway, Melanie decided. She had to get Christina to help her study for a civics test.

"Not again!" Christina said in a mock huffy voice. "And don't tell me you forgot about this test, too."

"I didn't. I was just really tired last night," Melanie said, which was partly true. After ponying Perfection, riding Trib, and practicing on Old Hay Bales, she really had been wiped out. "Ask me something, anything, and I'll prove to you I studied."

"Name four amendments to the constitution," Christina said promptly.

"Uh . . ." Melanie didn't have a clue. "Amendments. I don't think our class learned that."

Christina rolled her eyes. "If your class is studying chapter seven, then you learned about amendments."

"I must have been daydreaming that day." Melanie gave her cousin a sheepish smile.

Christina giggled. "Let me guess. Did it have something to do with winning the Kentucky Derby?"

"Probably." The bus bounced, tossing Melanie halfway into the aisle. She glanced over her shoulder. Kevin was laughing loudly at something Cassidy was saying.

"Have you noticed that Kevin's acting a little strange lately?" she asked Christina.

"You mean stranger than normal?" Christina joked. She was trying to pull her fat civics book from her backpack.

"Seriously. He seems—different."

"Different how?"

"I'm not sure. He seems mad about something. I hope he's not mad at me, but it does seem as if he doesn't like me anymore."

"He still likes you. Yesterday he asked me if I thought you'd like to go to the movies with him and Dylan and me this Saturday night." Christina opened her book.

"Really? Cool." *But why didn't he ask me this morning?* Melanie wondered. From the beginning, she and Kevin had hit it off. The one thing she really liked about him was how up-front he was about things.

"Even if he asks me, I might not be able to go. Your folks may race Heart of Stone this weekend, and I definitely want to be there."

"If Stone races, you'll still be home in time," Christina pointed out.

"Hey, why don't you come to the race, too?" Melanie suggested.

Christina shook her head. "No way. I'm going to help Samantha. She's working with that new yearling she bought at the auction."

"The gray one?"

"Uh-huh. I really like her."

"What did Sam name her?"

"Her registered name is Sweet Dreams. Sam's going to call her Dream."

"Wow. Sweet Dreams. Sterling Dream. Maybe they're related."

Christina laughed. "I doubt it. Dream is going to be twice as big as Sterling." She opened her civics book. "Ready to study?"

"I'd rather talk about horses." Melanie sighed and slumped back into the bus seat. Her stomach grumbled, and she realized that in the rush, she'd forgotten to eat breakfast—though it was just as well, since Ashleigh had made blueberry muffins, Melanie's favorite. She'd been really good the past week about watching what she ate, and she definitely didn't need any fattening muffins. As Naomi had told her, jockeys had to keep their weight down.

"So where were you this morning?" Christina's question broke into her thoughts. "Running alone was no fun."

Melanie flushed. "I'm sorry. I overslept. Won't happen again," she promised. Then she noticed the grin her cousin was trying to hold back. "Wait a minute. You didn't work out, either."

"Nope. And boy, did that extra half-hour feel good."

"Tonight we make it up, and tomorrow it's back to our routine, okay?"

Christina bit her lip. "I don't know, Mel, I—"

"No buts about it. Your week's not up." Reaching

over, Melanie squeezed Christina's arm muscle. "Look, you're getting stronger already."

"That's from hauling all these books around," Christina said, pointing to her backpack. "Maybe you should try it."

"Nah. I'm getting my homework done at school," Melanie insisted.

Christina gave her a skeptical look. "I hope so. Midterm progress reports come out the end of next week, you know."

"I know." Turning her head, Melanie looked across the aisle and out the other side of the window. She hated to lie to Christina. Not that her cousin hadn't already guessed the truth about Melanie and her schoolwork. But Christina was one of those kids who really enjoyed doing well at school and wouldn't understand.

Unlike me, Melanie thought. Not that she wanted to flunk eighth grade or anything. But her dad was used to lousy report cards, and Aunt Ashleigh would understand, since she hadn't been such a hot student, either.

Bored with worrying about school, Melanie let her mind wander to the great workout she'd had on Stoney. Since she'd done so well with him, she just knew that Mike would let her ride Perfection once he was sound. By then, she'd be in really good shape to handle the spirited colt.

Which means lots of hard work and no more sleeping in, Melanie reminded herself. The weekend was coming, and she'd get to ride as much as she wanted. It would be heaven.

For the next ten minutes Christina quizzed her on the amendments. When they got off the bus, they waited for Dylan, Kevin, and Katie. Cassidy stayed on the bus, since she went to the high school.

"Katie was telling us about an overnight trail ride that Mona's organizing for the weekend after next," Dylan told the two girls. "Mona has to come back Saturday night, so Samantha and Tor have agreed to go, too."

"Hey, sounds fun," Christina said. "Count me in."

"It's going to be sooo cool," Katie said. "The place we're staying has three cabins. One for the guys, one for the girls, and one for Tor and Sam."

"What about the horses?" Christina asked. "Where do they stay?"

"Mona said something about run-in sheds with paddocks."

The weekend after next. Melanie wondered what else would be going on that weekend. Stone probably wouldn't race again so soon. Still, did she want to give up two days of galloping racehorses for a trail ride with friends she saw almost every day?

As the group started down the sidewalk and into school, Kevin fell into step beside Melanie.

"Sounds fun, doesn't it?" he said.

Melanie nodded and smiled, wondering if he was really going to ask her to the movies. "I don't know if I can make the ride, though. Once Stone starts racing, they're probably going to want me to keep working with him."

"Oh, right," Kevin said sarcastically. "I forgot. The great jockey doesn't have time for her friends."

Melanie stopped dead, surprised by his tone. "That's not true and you know it."

He shrugged. "Oh, really? Not that I'll be able to make it, either. Basketball practice starts, and my dad expects me to work with those yearlings on the weekend." Suddenly he shook his head as if disturbed about something.

"Kevin, what's going on with you?" Melanie asked.

"Nothing's going on. Look, I've got to get to class." Without another word, he turned and disappeared into the crowd of kids.

Now Melanie was really confused. What was Kevin's problem, anyway? Going to her locker, she opened it and pulled out her books. If she hurried to class, she'd have a few minutes to review her civics notes.

"Good luck on your test," Christina said before she rushed down the hall to her homeroom.

"You too," Melanie called back.

Clutching her books in her arms, she slammed her locker door, then headed to class. Mr. Sykes was her homeroom teacher as well as her civics teacher. As he droned on about trying out for the eighth-grade choir, Melanie quickly scanned her notes, mentally reciting the dates, numbers, and content of the amendments.

I'm going to do okay, she told herself. But ten minutes later, when he handed out the test, the information she'd studied ran together in one big blur.

Melanie's stomach twisted into a knot. She might as well quit kidding herself. She was going to flunk this one.

6

"FIFTY, FIFTY-ONE, FIFTY-TWO," MELANIE COUNTED AS SHE did her sit-ups Saturday morning. It was nine o'clock. Already she'd jogged, ridden Trib, and galloped Shining Moment, and now she was ready to head to the Keeneland racetrack whenever Ashleigh said it was time.

"Fifty-three," Melanie gasped. She forced herself to do one more sit-up before collapsing on her back. Christina came down the stairs dressed in jeans and a sweatshirt.

"You haven't left yet?" she asked Melanie.

"Stone doesn't run until this afternoon. Ian and Naomi left with the van. I'm going with your mom." She struggled onto her elbows, and for a second her head swam dizzily. "Sure you don't want to come?"

"Positive. Every time I go to a racetrack it reminds

me of when I got Sterling." She grimaced. "And that awful groom who abused her. I don't need to see any more nasty people like that."

Holding up her arm, Melanie flexed her muscles. "Hey, I can handle them. I'm getting tougher."

Christina grinned. "I know, I know. But have you heard some of Naomi and Nathan's stories?"

Melanie shook her head.

"Ask them. Some jockeys will do anything to win," Christina said. "It can get pretty rough, Mel."

Anything. The word echoed in Melanie's ears long after Christina left. Obviously her cousin didn't think she had the guts to be a jockey.

"Fifty-five, fifty-six . . ." Melanie forced herself to do twenty more sit-ups. When she finally quit, her abdominal muscles ached.

"Melanie? Are you ready to go?" Ashleigh asked from the hallway. She wore tan corduroy pants and an off-white pullover sweater. Her hair was held back in a headband, making her look like a little kid.

Melanie scrambled to her feet. "Just let me grab my jacket."

A couple of minutes later she joined Ashleigh in the car. When they were headed down the drive, Melanie said, "So, Aunt Ashleigh, tell me about when you were riding Wonder."

Ashleigh made a face. "You don't really want me to go into all that. Besides, didn't you and Christina just finish going through all my old junk last week?"

"Yes, but the trophies and pictures of you in the winner's circle told only half the story. What about the other half, the bad times?"

"Why do you want to hear those awful stories?"

"Because if I'm going to be a jockey, I have to know everything," Melanie insisted.

"Well, you already know how easily a young Thoroughbred can injure itself. . . ." Her voice trailed off, and she stared out the windshield, her brow furrowed.

"Aunt Ashleigh?" Melanie prompted quietly.

Her aunt swung her head around as if startled. "Did you say something?"

"What were you thinking about just then?"

Ashleigh let out a heavy sigh. "I was just thinking back to when Wonder broke her cannon bone during a workout." She shook her head sadly. "That's when we had to retire her."

"Wow. That must have been tough on you," Melanie said. Her aunt nodded, and Melanie thought she saw tears in her eyes.

"No more sad stories. It might bring Whitebrook bad luck."

When they arrived at the racetrack, Ashleigh pulled into the parking lot behind the shed row. Both Heart of Stone and Leap of Faith were racing, so Whitebrook had three stalls—one for each horse and one for supplies.

They found Mike in the stall brushing Stone. Most farm owners had dozens of grooms and hotwalkers,

57

but Mike and Ashleigh believed in working as closely as they could with the horses.

"How's he feeling?" Ashleigh asked her husband.

"Nervous. Naomi warmed him up when we first got here this morning, so he got a chance to look around the track and the grandstand. Still, it will be a lot more confusing during the race."

Opening the door, Melanie went in to greet the big horse. She held both sides of the halter and looked him in the face. "You will not get distracted. You will pay attention to Naomi."

"Are you trying to hypnotize him?" Ashleigh asked with a laugh.

"If that's what it takes," Melanie said, grinning.

"Post time for Stone is one o'clock," Mike announced. "He's in the first race. Faith's in the third race. Ian's grooming her. Naomi's in the jockey room getting dressed and weighed."

Ashleigh checked her watch. "We'd better start getting them both ready. I'll help Ian."

Melanie gave Mike a hand putting on the bandages that would help protect Stone's lower legs and fetlocks. The Thoroughbred jogged in place. By the time he was tacked up and ready, his neck was already dark with patches of sweat.

"Can I help you take him to the paddocks?" Melanie asked her uncle. "Maybe a familiar face will calm him down."

"Think you can handle him?"

She nodded vigorously.

"Okay." He clipped a lead line onto Stone's bridle. "I'll be right beside you with the saddle."

As Melanie led Stone past the rows of stalls, he gazed wide-eyed at his surroundings. Reaching up, she scratched him on the mane, trying to reassure him that everything was all right. At the paddock gate, an official handed Melanie the number 4 to clip on Stone's bridle.

"That means he's fourth from the rail," Mike explained. "This is Heart of Stone," he told an inspector with a clipboard.

The woman lifted Stone's upper lip to check his registration tattoo against the number on her list. "Go on in," she said, already heading for the horse behind Stone.

"Walk him around the oval for a while," Mike told Melanie. "I'll meet you in the saddling stall."

Melanie held the lead lightly, letting Stone look at all the confusion around him. He danced for a few strides, but as she soothed him with her voice and he settled into a long, swinging walk.

When all the horses were in the paddock, Melanie glanced around. She could see a skinny chestnut with wild eyes, a small bay whose ears were laid back in anger, and a fidgety black dragging a tall man.

"You're the handsomest, smartest horse here," Melanie whispered to Stone as she stroked his neck. Her heart filled with excitement and pride. She'd been to the track before, but this was totally different. If Stone won, she'd feel as though she was part of it.

When she passed by their assigned saddling stall, Mike gestured for her to bring the horse in. They saddled him, smoothing the blanket with the number 4 on it so it was flat on his back. Naomi came over wearing blue-and-white racing silks. Goggles were perched on top of her helmet, which had a blue cover. The number 4 was on the top of her right sleeve.

Melanie gave her an excited hug. "I think he's ready!" she told her.

"He'd better be, because I'm really nervous," Naomi said. "When I raced Faith, there were only five horses. This field is a lot bigger. That means lots of jostling and jockeying for the rail."

"You can handle it," Mike said. "Just remember—"

"To keep him focused on the race," Melanie finished her uncle's sentence. "Only you don't have to use the whip. Just urge him with your voice and body. And watch out, he likes to swing wide around the bend, so keep your left rein on him and—"

When she paused to take a breath, Mike said with a laugh, "I think Naomi knows what to do."

"Riders up!" the paddock judge hollered.

Melanie led Stone from the stall. He pranced in place, his neck arched. "He definitely knows what he's here for," Melanie told Naomi.

Mike gave Naomi a leg up. When she was settled in the saddle, Melanie walked beside her until they were outside the paddock. Then horse and rider joined the line of other horses for the parade to the track.

Tears of excitement filled Melanie's eyes. "I'm going to watch," she told Mike.

"I'll check on Faith, then join you."

Melanie hurried to the open area in front of the grandstand and found a spot along the rail. The horses were trotting and cantering up the track. Melanie spotted Stone. His bay coat glistened in the sun; his muscles rippled. Everyone could see he was fit and ready. She checked the odds on him. Five to two. The bettors must have liked him as well, despite the fact that this was his first race.

As they loaded the horses into the gate, Melanie's heart started to thump. Stone went in quietly, but the horse next to him, in the number five position, reared and backed out. Finally the starters had them all loaded. A slight hush fell over the crowd.

Then the bell rang and the gates flew open. "And they're off!" the announcer called.

Melanie stood on tiptoe, trying to find Stone in the galloping herd. Suddenly Mike and Ashleigh were behind her. Mike had binoculars trained on the field.

"Where is he? Where is he?" Melanie muttered as she jumped up and down. Then they thundered past, and she caught sight of Naomi's blue helmet cover in the middle of the pack. Melanie whooped. "They're on the rail! Right where they should be!"

"She's just got to move him up. Now!" Ashleigh said, her voice tense.

The horses raced to the other side of the track in a tight pack.

"Uncle Mike, may I use the binoculars?" Melanie asked as they came around the last bend. "I've got to see how he's doing."

He handed them to her, and she trained them on the field as the horses headed for the finish line. Her heart caught in her throat. Stone was in the front, battling for first place with three other horses.

Melanie dropped the binoculars to her chest. "Go, Stoney, go!" she whispered. Hands in front of her, she automatically pumped in rhythm to his stride. Naomi crouched low on the big horse's neck, and Melanie could almost hear her urge him on with everything she had. The bay's stride lengthened, and with a final burst of speed, he inched away from the other horses and crossed the finish line first. Stone had won! Melanie could hardly believe it.

Together Mike, Melanie, and Ashleigh let out a whoop. The crowd roared its approval. Melanie hugged Ashleigh, then grabbed Mike's hand and danced in a circle. "He did it!"

"Come to the winner's circle with us," Ashleigh said, linking arms with her.

They hurried through the crowd. The outrider was trotting next to Stone as he paraded to the winner's circle.

Naomi was grinning. "He did great!" she told Mike, Ashleigh, and Melanie when they came up.

Melanie snapped the lead shank onto Stone's bridle,

then threw her arms around his sweaty neck. "Good job, Stoney!"

"Hey, Mel, smile for the cameras," Mike said, pointing toward a crowd of reporters and photographers. An official handed Naomi a trophy while the journalists shouted questions and snapped pictures.

Melanie led Stone from the winner's circle, and Naomi dismounted. "How'd your second win feel?" Melanie asked her.

"Like I'm still thirty-three wins away from being a real jockey." Naomi pulled off her helmet. Her chin and cheeks were splattered with dirt. "Actually, it felt great."

Just then a man and woman came over. "Nice race," they told the two girls. "Handsome horse."

Turning to Ashleigh and Mike, the man stuck out his hand and introduced himself. "I'm Jeff Owens, and this is my wife, Sarilee. We're interested in buying your horse."

Melanie had been loosening Stone's girth. When she heard him, she swung around in surprise. "Stone's not for sale," she said.

As if Mike hadn't heard her, he shook the man's hand. "Nice to meet you both."

Jeff patted the horse's wet neck. "I like your colt, plus I hear your farm has an excellent reputation for producing fast, intelligent racehorses."

"You're the Owenses who own Rushing Creek Farms?" Ashleigh asked.

When the man nodded, Ashleigh went on, "I know your head trainer, Ben Cavell. He used to work in Virginia. I heard he came to Kentucky. He's a good trainer. If we do sell Heart of Stone to you, he'll be in good hands."

Melanie's mouth dropped open. Was she hearing right? Would Ashleigh and Mike even consider selling him?

"I think we can make an offer you can't refuse," Sarilee said. "We're a racing stable, so we're interested in geldings with long-term racing potential. This guy's got the head and heart we're looking for."

Mike glanced down at Ashleigh, who nodded. "I think we can talk. We have a filly in the third race. Why don't we meet you after that?"

"Done." The four shook hands again. Melanie was so stunned, she couldn't say anything.

"Mel, you better'd start walking him," Mike said. "Put the cooler on him before he stiffens up in this chilly air."

"B-But . . . ," Melanie stammered, "you just told those people you might sell Stone to them!"

Mike cocked one brow as if puzzled by her reaction. "That's right."

Melanie glanced from Mike to Ashleigh, and she could tell from the expressions on their faces that they didn't get it. She loved Stone. They couldn't just sell him.

"We would have sold him sooner or later," Ashleigh

64

explained. "That's part of our business, Melanie. Training racehorses to sell—for the right price, of course."

"That's right, Mel." Mike chucked her on the shoulder. "If the Owenses' make a good offer, Stone won't be going back with us to Whitebrook."

7

IN A DAZE, MELANIE WALKED HEART OF STONE UNDER THE overhangs of the shed row. Horses, grooms, hotwalkers, and trainers went past in noisy confusion, but she didn't notice.

She'd been so naive. She should have known the horse would be sold. Mike and Ashleigh ran a business. They couldn't keep every horse they owned.

Kevin was right. She was lucky they'd kept Pirate around the farm.

At least Melanie knew that if the Owenses did buy Stone, he'd be going to a great place. Ashleigh had assured her that he'd get the best of care and training under Ben Cavell.

A tear trickled down her cheek. Was this what Kevin and Christina meant about being tough enough for the racing business? Good jockeys rode hundreds of different horses. It was their job to ride them to win; they couldn't get attached to them.

Stopping Stone, Melanie felt under his blanket. He was still warm, but cool enough for a sip of water. As she led him to the bucket outside his stall, she heard a roar from the grandstand. Then the announcer said, "The winner is Leap of Faith, owned by Whitebrook Farms, ridden by Naomi Traeger."

Melanie's heart swelled with pride. Two wins in one day! Naomi was doing great. She bet other trainers were taking notice. Soon they'd be asking Mike and Ashleigh if Naomi could ride for them. She'd have to get an agent, and her career as a jockey would be launched.

Outside the stall, Stoney lowered his head and took several gulps of water. "That's enough, big guy." Melanie lifted his head, then headed in the opposite direction. Two more turns around the backstretch, and he'd probably be cool. Then she'd have to wrap up his legs for the trip home.

She caught herself. If the Owenses bought him, he wouldn't be going home.

Twenty minutes later Ian came striding back leading Faith. The gray filly was still in high spirits from the race and he had to hold her tight. Several grooms and trainers who knew Ian stopped to slap him on the back.

"Congratulations," Melanie said, falling into step beside them.

"She ran a terrific race." Ian's voice was filled with

pride. "Mike was right when he took a chance on her. She's a winner."

Melanie glanced around. "Are Mike and Ashleigh talking with the Owenses?"

Ian nodded. "Now, don't you worry," he said when he halted Faith outside her stall. "Heart of Stone will be going to a good stable with good hands."

He pulled the saddle off Faith, and the horse skittered sideways. "Still got plenty of race left in her." He chuckled. "This is one filly Mike won't part with."

"I bet you've seen plenty of horses come and go," Melanie said.

"More than I can count. That's why—" He stopped abruptly and busied himself with taking off Faith's bridle and putting on her halter.

"Why what?" Melanie asked.

"Nothing. At least nothing I can talk about right now. You'd better settle down, Faith, or I'll be walking you around all night," he scolded the filly as he slipped the chain under her jaw.

Melanie's curiosity was piqued, but she figured Ian wasn't going to say any more. She took Stone around for one more lap. When he was cool enough, she folded back the blanket to his withers and headed back to the stall. Jeff Owens and a short, bald guy with a gut hanging over his belt were talking with Mike. The short guy had a lead line in his hand.

Melanie's heart plummeted. They'd come for Heart of Stone.

She halted Stone and turned to slip her arms around his neck. She buried her face in his shoulder. Hot tears filled her eyes. "This is it, Stoney," she whispered. "This is goodbye."

Stepping back, she wiped her eyes with the sleeve of her jacket. She wasn't going to let anyone see her tears. She'd show them she could handle it.

"There he is, Ben," Mr. Owens said when she led the big colt over to them.

The short guy rocked back on the heels of his cowboy boots. "Nice." Bending, he ran his hands down Stone's front legs. "Real nice."

Melanie watched, noticing that the man's touch was gentle. As he walked around, he talked in a quiet voice.

Melanie's stomach unknotted a little. Stone would be going to a good barn.

"He's really a great horse," she piped up.

"Melanie's been his exercise rider," Mike said. "She's done a great job with him."

"He's like a big kid that needs lots of attention and leg to keep him focused," she continued, feeling bolder. "But not the whip."

Ben raised his bushy brows. "Sounds like good advice." He snapped his lead to Stone's halter. Taking a deep breath, Melanie unsnapped hers, then unbuckled the blue and white cooler and pulled it off.

"I'll take him to the barn," Ben told Mr. Owens, and, turning, he led Stone down the aisle.

Melanie watched them leave, her heart aching. But

she swallowed the sob that welled in her throat, and busily began folding the cooler.

Mike came over. "Are you all right?"

Afraid to say anything, she nodded, then hurried into Stone's stall. There was a lot to do before they could go home.

Mike came in and stood in the doorway. "Naomi's riding in the fifth race on one of the Owenses' horses. They were quite impressed with her riding. I think they're going to ask her to continue to race Stone. You'll be able to see him anytime you're here."

"Good." She cleared her throat as she unsnapped his feed bucket. "It won't be the same, though. I really loved galloping him."

"I know. But hey, we have five coming two-year-olds who need lots of work. Think you're up to it?"

Biting her lip to hold back the tears, she nodded again.

"Good. Now let's go watch Naomi win another race."

Melanie was silent that afternoon as she rode home with Ashleigh and Naomi. In the front seat, Naomi was chattering excitedly, keyed up by two wins and a place. Ashleigh was almost as excited as they discussed future plans for Faith.

Slumping in the backseat, Melanie sighed heavily. She was amazed that Stone's sale hadn't affected them more. Melanie really admired both Naomi and Ashleigh. If she was going to be like them, she'd have to toughen up. She couldn't grieve over every horse that left Whitebrook.

"Ian and Mike are bringing Faith home, then leaving again with the van," Ashleigh was saying. "Melanie, can you help Naomi get Faith settled for the night?"

"Sure. Where are Ian and Mike going?"

"To pick up a horse. Sam and Ian bought a two-year-old racer—they went in on it together. You two are the first ones to know about it, after me."

"Really? Why were they so secretive about it?" Melanie demanded.

"They've been discussing whether to do it for a couple of days. Beth and Tor weren't as keen on the idea as Sam and Ian." Tor was Sam's husband, and Beth was Ian's wife and Kevin's mother.

"Why not? Those two are great with racehorses."

"The colt cost a lot of money. Tor's worried because their own farm is just getting off the ground. Beth's worried because Ian cleaned out their savings. And you know how risky racehorses are."

"Has the horse raced?" Melanie asked.

"Not yet. He's never been ridden. He's got super bloodlines, though. Traces back to Secretariat," Ashleigh said. She smiled at Melanie in the rearview mirror. "They'll keep him at Whitebrook, and Ian and Sam will train him together. They're bringing him back tonight."

Melanie sat forward in her seat. "Sounds like they'll need a groom for him," she said.

Ashleigh chuckled. "Yup, sounds like they will."

When they reached Whitebrook, Melanie ran to the barn to see Pirate. The black horse was turned out in the pasture with several yearlings. When he heard her, he trotted over to the fence. Climbing up, Melanie sat on the top board and scratched under his forelock. "Thank goodness you're still here."

A gawky colt came over and to see what was going on. Pirate laid back his ears and gave him a stern look, and the colt raced away and up the hill. Melanie laughed. "You're like a grumpy old father."

Father—that was what she needed to do that night, call her dad. It had been too long since she'd spoken to him.

Melanie heard the rumble of the van as it came up the drive. Jumping off the fence, she ran to meet it. Naomi was exhausted and had gone home, but Maureen would still be around to help her with Faith.

By the time Faith was unloaded, the filly's neck was covered with sweat. "She banged the whole ride," Ian said as he checked her over for bumps. Maureen had joined Melanie, and Mike explained what they needed to do to settle her for the night.

"Now that she's home, she'll probably calm down. She's going to need lots of walking, though, and check her legs for swelling. Also, a light feed tonight. We

72

should be back in an hour with Wind Chaser."

Wind Chaser. Melanie liked the name. She glanced over at Ian, who was bustling around, pulling things from the van. She wondered if Samantha was going with them.

After they left, Melanie bathed Faith, then walked her. Jonnie was feeding, and Maureen was working in the office, so Melanie was on her own with Faith.

Back on her own turf, the filly soon quieted. Melanie gave her a brisk rubdown, then walked her some more. By the time Maureen took over, Melanie was dragging her feet with exhaustion.

"Better get some dinner," Maureen said. "Ian and Sam's horse should be here soon."

"Good idea." Melanie ran to the house. Ashleigh and Christina were in the kitchen, discussing the day. Christina was dressed in jeans and an emerald green knit top. Her hair had been blown dry and she looked like she was going out. "Hey, Mel," she said. "Ready to go to the movies with us?"

Melanie clapped a hand over her mouth. "What movies? Did I forget something?" she asked.

"Kevin never asked you?" Christina demanded.

Melanie shook her head. "No. I figured you guys weren't going, either."

"We're going to the early show so we can go to Mona's afterward to talk about the weekend trail ride. She's going to have pizza and stuff."

"Oh." Melanie didn't know what to say. She glanced

down at her jeans and mud-stained jacket. "How about if I meet you at Mona's? Ashleigh, would you drive me?"

"I'm sure someone around here can give you a ride," Ashleigh said.

"Meet you there, then," Christina said. A horn beeped outside. "Dylan's mom is here." Christina grabbed her windbreaker from the back of the kitchen chair. After pecking her mom on the cheek, she ran out.

"Is Kevin going?" Melanie hollered after her. But all she heard was the slam of the front door.

"I think Kevin had a late afternoon basketball practice," Ashleigh said. "How about a slice of veggie lasagna?"

"Uncle Mike ate veggie lasagna?"

Ashleigh laughed. "No way. I fixed a special one for you." She held up a cardboard box from a frozen dinner. "Mama Mia's own recipe."

Melanie grinned. "I was wondering when you had the time to make lasagna." After washing her hands, she sat down at the table, ate a few bites, and raced upstairs to shower. She wanted to be ready by the time they arrived with Wind Chaser.

Melanie was putting on her sweater when she heard the van rumble past the house. Slipping on her muddy paddock boots, she raced after it.

Ian parked in front of the training barn and got out. Samantha and Mike climbed out the other side. Samantha was grinning from ear to ear. Ian still looked nervous.

"How'd he ride?" Melanie asked.

"A perfect gentlemen," Samantha gushed. "In fact, he is perfect in every way."

"Gee, I can't wait to see this million-dollar guy," a voice said beside Melanie. Kevin had come up next to her. He wore a clean sweatshirt and jeans, and his hair was still damp, as if he'd just gotten out of the shower.

As Ian and Mike lowered the ramp, Melanie stared excitedly at the side opening. A whinny rang from the van.

When the ramp was lowered, Samantha strode up it. "Hey, handsome," Melanie could hear her croon. She looked sideways at Kevin. She was surprised to see that he was frowning.

"You're not excited about the new horse?" she asked him.

He shrugged. "No one asked my opinion about buying him. Not that they needed to. After all, it's not my money, right?"

He said the last sentence in such an angry voice, Melanie wasn't sure what to say. Was Wind Chaser the reason Kevin had to earn extra money for the basketball clinic?

The clomp of hooves made Melanie glance back at the van. Samantha was leading Wind Chaser down the ramp. When the horse got to the bottom, he pranced in a circle, and Melanie's eyes widened.

Wind Chaser didn't look like a typical two-year-old. He was over sixteen hands, filled-out and sleek, with rippling muscles in his chest and hindquarters. He was an unusual color, too—golden chestnut with a flaxen mane and tail. His brown eyes gazed at his new home with interest, and when he swung around, Melanie could see the intelligence in his expression.

"Wow," Melanie gasped. "That is the most awesome colt I've ever seen!"

"I think so, too." Samantha stepped back to show off the new arrival. "What do you think, Kevin?"

He was still standing beside Melanie, his hands stuck in his back jeans pockets as if he couldn't care less. But Melanie could see a hint of interest in his eyes.

"Nice." Kevin shrugged. "But I think you need to get Mom down here and show her. She's the one who wasn't too happy about you guys buying such an expensive horse."

Ian's gaze darted up the hill toward the cottage where the McLeans lived. "Good idea, Kevin," he said. "Sam, can you get him settled while I go get Beth?"

"I'll help!" Melanie practically shouted.

Mike laughed. "I think someone's got her eyes on this guy," he teased.

She flushed. "All right, I'll admit it. I've never seem anything like him. Of course, I know I'm not experienced enough to ride him," she added, hoping someone would disagree.

"We'll see. I'm going to walk him awhile and let him settle down," Samantha said as she led Chaser toward the barn.

We'll see! Melanie's heart skipped a beat. That meant she might have a chance.

"No way are you going to be Chaser's groom," Kevin said abruptly when Samantha was out of earshot. "Chaser belongs to us. So you can forget about being his groom or riding him, Melanie. That's going to be my job."

8

WHAT WAS KEVIN TALKING ABOUT? AND WHY DID HE HAVE to be so mean? "Chaser belongs to Samantha and your dad," she retorted. "Not you. They'll decide who gets to work with him."

"And they'll pick me," Kevin declared. "I'm more experienced and a better rider."

Melanie clenched her fists by her sides. "Oh, really?" she challenged, stepping close enough that Kevin had to look down at her. "I've been working really hard these past months, and Sam and Ian know it. I bet they'll pick me."

"We'll see," Kevin said. For a second the two glared at each other. Then Mike came down the van's ramp carrying a hay net.

"What are you two arguing about?" he asked.

"Nothing," Melanie said quickly, stepping back.

"We were uh . . . just talking about going over to Mona's tonight."

Mike wrinkled his forehead in disbelief. "Is that so?"

"Ashleigh said she'd drive me over later," Melanie continued. "Everybody's meeting to talk about next weekend's trail ride."

"I thought you weren't going on the ride," Kevin said.

"I might go now that Stoney was sold," Melanie said, feeling a pang of sadness.

"Good. I'll stay here and work with Chaser," Kevin said, grinning triumphantly.

Melanie put her hands on her hips. "Oh, no you won't."

"Hey, would you two stop arguing?" Mike broke in. "You sound like a couple of two-year-olds fighting over a toy. Believe me, there are plenty of horses—and work— to go around."

But there's only one Chaser, Melanie thought.

Just then Melanie heard the clop of hooves. She turned and watched Samantha walk down the aisle with the new colt. He had a stripe down his face and three white socks. His eyes were huge, and his nostrils flared as he took in the sights and smells.

"He is something," she told Samantha.

"That's for sure," Samantha agreed. She halted Chaser in front of Melanie and Kevin. "He seems so smart and aware, too. If he's got the heart and desire to win, he'll be unbeatable."

"You mean, if he wants to win just as much we want him to?" Melanie asked. "Can a horse really want to win like that?"

"Well, a keen horse will see an opening along the rail and go for it without the jockey's even telling him," Samantha explained. "A lot of jumpers have that kind of savvy over fences because they're older and wiser when they start campaigning seriously. It's more unusual to see it in a younger colt like him."

"How do you know that this horse will have that kind of smarts?" Kevin asked, sounding skeptical. "Dad always said when you buy a young horse, it's a gamble. You two could lose every cent you put into him."

Samantha shrugged. "You're right. It is a gamble. Chaser could decide he hates racing. We'll just have to keep our fingers crossed."

"I think he'll be a winner." Stepping closer, Melanie stroked Chaser's silky neck. He lowered his head and snuffled the front of her shirt.

"May I walk him to the end of the barn, Sam?" Melanie asked. "I'll introduce him to some of the other horses."

"Sure." Samantha handed her the lead line. Melanie grasped it carefully. When she led Chaser away, she could feel the power radiate from his body, yet his walk was light and balanced.

Behind her, she heard Samantha say, "Kevin, I hope you and Beth will understand why Dad and I bought this horse."

Melanie strained her ears, trying to hear Kevin's response, but she was too far away. She bet that in a minute he'd ask Samantha about being Chaser's groom.

Well, there was no way! Melanie just had to work with him, especially now that Stone was gone.

"What does Kevin know, anyway?" she asked Chaser.

Maybe Kevin did have a teeny point about how Chaser belonged to his family. But she didn't see Beth rushing out and demanding to groom the horse. Besides, she told herself, it was Kevin's I-could-care-less-about-you attitude that really made her mad.

In fact, she didn't think Kevin really wanted to work with Chaser at all. He'd barely looked at the horse. It was as if he was deliberately trying to keep Melanie from being Chaser's groom. Why would he want to do that?

Melanie really didn't care why. All she knew was how much she wanted to be the colt's groom. She would convince Sam and Ian that she was the right one for the job.

Stopping Chaser in front of Pirate's stall, she introduced the two. Pirate came up to the door, and the two horses touched noses. Melanie figured they'd probably squeal and make a fuss. When they didn't, Melanie patted Chaser.

"Pirate will be your pony horse," she told him. "He can be bossy, but he'll take care of you."

Chaser rubbed his head on her shoulder, then

lipped her hair. Instantly she forgot about Stone, Kevin, Christina, and the trail ride. All she could think about was the horse beside her, and how desperately she wanted to have a part in his training.

When she turned to walk back down the aisle, she noticed Kevin was gone. This might be her only chance to talk to Samantha.

"Can I be his groom, Sam, please?" Melanie pleaded. "I really think I could do a great job. You know how hard I've been working, and now that Stone's gone I'll have time for another horse."

Samantha grinned at her. "I knew you'd like him. I'll have to check with Mike and Ian, but as far as I'm concerned, you've got the job."

"Yes!" Melanie punched the air, startling the horse. Chaser backed up a step and stared at her as if she was crazy.

"Don't look at me like that," Melanie said to him, laughing. "I didn't mean to scare you. I'm just excited that I'm going to take care of you. Who cares if Kevin doesn't like it? Once Ian and Sam see how wonderful I am with you, it won't be long until I'm your exercise rider, too."

Everybody was sitting around Mona's family room digging into the snacks. Dylan, Katie, Parker, and Christina had arrived from the movies only minutes before Ashleigh had dropped off Melanie.

"Wait'll you guys see Wind Chaser!" Melanie gushed. "He's gorgeous. He's got beautiful big eyes, and he's this gold color with a white stripe down his nose. His stride is huge—"

"He sounds great, Melanie," Katie interrupted. "But do you mind if you tell us about Chaser a little later? My dad's coming in half an hour and we need to figure out who's going to get which supplies for the trail ride."

"Oh." Melanie picked up a piece of gooey cheese pizza and took a bite.

"As I was saying," Katie went on, "we'll each need to bring some of the food and supplies. Dylan, why don't you bring . . ."

As Katie chattered on about marshmallows and hot dogs, Melanie's mind wandered. It had been such an exciting day. Just by spending the day at Keeneland she'd learned so many new things about racing. It was sad to see Stone go, but she realized that selling him was all part of the big picture of breeding, raising, and training winning racehorses. And she needed to focus on the big picture if she was going to become a jockey.

Suddenly she stopped chewing and stared at the pizza slice in her hand. She'd already eaten dinner. Why was she eating fattening pizza?

Mona came in from the kitchen carrying mugs of hot chocolate on a tray. She was dressed in her usual jeans and an oversized sweater, and her dark hair was a tangle of fly-away curls. Mona always chose comfort over fashion, and her house was the same way. Before the kids had arrived, she'd built a fire that was burning brightly.

Mona Gardener was Ashleigh's best friend, and had been Christina's riding instructor for years. Katie still kept her horse, Seabreeze, at Gardener Farm, but at Mona's suggestion, Christina, and now Dylan, had started working with Samantha and Tor at Whisperwood. Parker boarded his mare, Foxy, at Whisperwood, too, and as soon as his broken arm healed, he'd begin taking lessons again.

When Mona started passing around the hot chocolate, Melanie declined. "No, thanks. If I get thirsty, I'll get a glass of water."

"Melanie, why don't you contribute drinks?" Katie suggested as she went down her list. "Those boxed juices may be the best."

Melanie shook her head. "Sorry. I've decided not to go on the ride. Too much to do next weekend."

"Like what? I mean, I know it can't be homework you're doing," Katie said. "Since you haven't handed in a paper in English in weeks."

Melanie frowned. "I have, too, and besides, what business is it of yours what I do in school?"

Katie flushed pink. "I was only making a—"

"I'll bring the drinks," Dylan cut in.

"Thanks, Dylan. It's not that I don't want to go with you guys," Melanie explained, hoping she hadn't hurt anyone's feelings. "But I think I'm going to be

Chaser's groom, which means I shouldn't be away a whole weekend."

"I thought Kevin was going to be his groom," Christina said. "That's what he told me."

"Well, he's wrong," Melanie stated firmly. "Actually, Sam and Ian haven't decided yet."

Katie looked puzzled. "Why are you and Kevin fighting over being a groom? It's just a lot of hard work."

"Maybe, but it's an excuse to spend more time in the barn, and it's a good way to learn stuff, too," Melanie explained. "Besides, if I do a good job, they may let me be his exercise rider."

"That's kind of what I'm doing at Whisperwood," Parker chimed in. "Being a working student isn't glamorous, but I'm learning tons about managing a barn and caring for horses."

Mona nodded in agreement. "Riding is only a small part of being a horse person. The daily care is the most important thing a person can learn."

"Of course, if I really want to be a jockey, I have to work on my riding, too," Melanie continued. "Which is what I need to be doing next weekend as well."

"Well, we'll miss you," Christina said before turning back to Katie. Katie handed out more assignments, and everybody started talking about the weekend again.

Jumping up from her seat, Melanie went into the kitchen. She was sorry she had come now that she had definitely decided not to go on the ride. She wished she were back at Whitebrook with Samantha and Wind

Chaser. Or hanging around Ashleigh and Mike and listening to stories about the track.

Melanie poured herself a glass of water. When she went back into the family room, she asked Mona if she could go out to the barn. She hadn't seen Mona's horses in ages.

"Sure," Mona said. "Just make sure you turn out the lights when you're done."

As she slipped on her jacket, Melanie could feel her friends' eyes on her. She knew they must wonder what was wrong. There was no way she could make them understand that she'd rather groom Chaser and muck out his stall then go on an overnight ride with them.

When she went outside, the cold night air felt good after the hot family room. The outside floodlight on the end of the barn made it easy to see. Melanie walked over to Mona's riding ring. The light cast shadows over the jumps, making them look huge. It seemed like ages since Melanie had ridden in the ring, taking a lesson on Trib with the others. In reality, it had been only a couple of weeks.

Had she changed that much since then?

Melanie leaned on the railing around the ring. She used to dream about jumping perfect courses. Now the ring and the jumps vanished, and the only thing she could imagine was a horse galloping around a track, Melanie perched in the saddle, urging him on.

Yes, Melanie thought with a sigh, she had definitely changed.

9

SUNDAY MORNING MELANIE WAS THE FIRST ONE UP. THE horses in training had a day off, but there were still plenty of chores to do. Besides, she wanted to beat Kevin to the barn.

Grabbing an apple for breakfast, she headed out the door. The sun was up, but it was still cold. Melanie shivered. She hadn't dressed warmly enough. She debated about running back to the house, then noticed that the lights were on in the McLeans' cottage.

She quickened her pace. George Ballard's pickup truck was parked in front of the stallion barn. George managed the farm's stallions. Hurrying, she made it to the training barn before anyone else. Since no one was around, she knew she shouldn't take Chaser out, but there was no reason she couldn't brush him in his stall. She wanted to prove to Samantha that she was the right choice to be Chaser's groom.

Heading for the tack room, she grabbed a grooming box and hurried to Chaser's stall. When she saw him, she stopped dead in her tracks. He was as gorgeous as she remembered.

"How was your first night at Whitebrook?" she asked. When she opened the door, he stood calmly. Melanie was impressed by his manners. So many of the colts and fillies were hyper and hard to handle.

"Wait until Christina sees you," Melanie said as she patted him. "She'll think you're just as gorgeous as I do."

Figuring the colt must be hungry, she brought him a flake of hay to munch while she worked. Then she unbuckled the blanket straps and pulled the blanket off. Melanie hummed happily as she brushed his golden coat.

Sundays were the best, she decided. No major routine. No school. She could hang out in the barns with the horses to her heart's content.

Of course, she did need to squeeze in workout and jogging time, and she wanted to keep practicing on Old Hay Bales, too. Maybe she could get to them when her barn chores were done.

Half an hour later she was finished grooming Chaser. Stepping back, she admired her handiwork. His tail was brushed full, his mane lay flat, and his coat glistened.

She heard the crunch of tires on gravel, then the

slam of a car door. "Hello?" she called, and a second later Samantha called back.

All right! Melanie grinned. Her plan was working. Samantha would see how dedicated she would be.

"Come see your new horse," Melanie called.

When Samantha peered in the stall, she gave a low whistle. "Hey, looks like you're taking this groom stuff pretty seriously."

"That's because I *am* serious," Melanie insisted. "I brushed every hair. He's so well behaved."

"He was hand-raised by Jeannine Bank, a friend of mine," Samantha explained. "She worked with him from birth."

Melanie frowned. "Why'd she sell him?"

"Several reasons. She didn't have the facilities or know-how to train him for racing. And money, of course. Her husband got sick and they had a lot of hospital bills. And she knew Chaser was going to the best farm in Kentucky."

"Wow. It sounds like a plot from the movie of the week."

Walking around Chaser, Samantha checked him over. "He looks great. I came early to brush him, but you beat me to it. Ashleigh, Tor, and Beth are coming to see him after breakfast. He's going to knock their socks off."

"Why were Tor and Beth so nervous about buying him?" Melanie asked.

Samantha shrugged. "Chaser's a big investment,

and Dad used almost all the family's savings."

"Wow. That's kind of a big deal. What about Tor?"

Samantha wrinkled her nose. "Fortunately, he's the one who does the books in our family, so it's his job to worry. Not that I blame him. Starting up our new farm has been expensive. We didn't really need a new horse on top of all the other responsibilities. But when Jeannine offered me Chaser and I went to see him, I fell in love with him."

"Well, as soon as Tor and Beth see how great he looks right now, they'll fall in love with him, too," Melanie said.

After putting the colt's blanket back on, Melanie went to brush Pirate. By then, Jonnie was starting to feed, and a ripple of excitement raced up and down the barn. Horses banged stall doors, kicked walls, and rattled feed tubs.

Pirate stood alertly, gazing out over the stall door as if he could see. When Jonnie got closer, he bellowed loudly. Melanie figured the blind horse could tell where Jonnie was by the sound of his footsteps.

"I already gave Chaser one flake of hay," she told Jonnie when he opened the door to give Pirate his grain. He nodded, then hurried to the next stall.

While Pirate ate, Melanie finished brushing him. Then she headed down the aisle to groom Perfection. On the way, she passed Stone's empty stall. She stopped and looked inside. Monday, Jonnie would clean and disinfect it. It wouldn't take long for a new horse to occupy it. *Maybe even this week sometime*, Melanie guessed, *when the yearlings are moved to the training barn*.

Melanie wondered if Stone missed his old barn. Had he spent a nervous night at the track? The busy backside would definitely have different smells and noises. She hoped he hadn't been too miserable.

With a sigh, she went down to Perfection's stall. The rangy colt was polishing off his hay. Melanie checked his legs. They felt cool, with no sign of puffiness.

"Won't be long before I start riding you again," she told him. "And watch out. This time I'll be ready for your shenanigans."

She was about to start brushing him when she heard a car drive up. Her heart quickened. Tor must have arrived to see Chaser. She wondered if Ashleigh, Christina, and the others were coming, too.

"I'll brush you later," she told Perfection before heading out. By the time she jogged from the barn, a crowd had gathered. Tor was talking to Ian, Ashleigh, Beth, and Mike. Christina was standing by her mother, her head resting on Ashleigh's arm.

Melanie glanced around, wondering where Samantha was. She heard voices behind her. Turning, she spotted Samantha and Kevin outside Chaser's stall. Kevin had a lead rope.

Fists clenched by her sides, Melanie strode down the aisle. After all her hard work, he wasn't going to lead out her horse!

Chaser's not your horse, Melanie corrected herself. *So*

calm down before you make a fool of yourself.

By the time she reached Chaser's stall, she was smiling pleasantly. "Need help?"

"Nope." Kevin handed the lead to Samantha, who went into Chaser's stall. He didn't even look at her.

"I feel like the royal guard presenting the new prince," Samantha said, sounding nervous. Taking off the colt's blanket, she handed it to Kevin.

"He's just a horse," Kevin said.

"He is not just a horse," Melanie retorted. How could Kevin not see how special Wind Chaser was?

"That's for sure. He's a big investment." Samantha smoothed the colt's coat with a soft cloth, then took a deep breath. "Well, here goes. Come on, handsome." She clucked, and he followed her from the stall and down the aisle like a big puppy dog.

For a second Melanie panicked. When she'd seen Chaser the night before, he was excited about being at his new home. Now he seemed too quiet and docile. What if everybody decided he didn't have enough spirit to be a racehorse?

Fingers crossed, she jogged down the aisle after them. Kevin had gone on ahead to join the others. When Samantha appeared in the doorway with the horse, Kevin made a trumpeting sound. "Introducing his majesty, Wind Chaser," he announced.

Everybody turned to watch as Samantha led the colt toward the group. Even George Ballard had joined them.

Melanie studied their faces, trying to judge their reactions. For a second no one did or said anything. And no wonder—the colt ambled along like an old school horse. Then suddenly he halted. Ears pricked alertly, he gazed around him, taking in the new sights. The sun gleamed off his satiny gold coat, and he looked so elegant that Melanie had to catch her breath.

Raising his head high, he let out a bellow that rang across the farm, and everyone starting talking at once.

"He's gorgeous!"

"He reminds me of Mr. Wonderful!"

Mr. Wonderful was Whitebrook's prized sire. When he was three, Ashleigh had ridden him to victory in both the Kentucky Derby and the Preakness. With his hulking shoulders and elegant air, Chaser did look a lot like him.

"Look at that conformation!"

"I knew Sam had good taste," Tor said. Coming over to Samantha, he put his arm around her and gave her a kiss on the cheek. "You guys did good."

Samantha beamed, and even Beth was smiling like a kid who'd gotten a new present. Melanie felt like sagging to the ground in relief.

"No wonder you wanted to talk about him last night," Christina said, coming up to Melanie. "He is something." She grinned, a gleam in her eyes. "Maybe when Sterling's too old to event, I'll breed her to him. What a match. What color do you think their foals would be?"

93

"Gray and gold make . . . uh . . . pink. Your favorite color," Melanie joked, and they both started laughing.

For a few minutes Samantha led Chaser around so everyone could admire him. Melanie noticed that Kevin hung back from the others. His arms were crossed in front of him, and his mouth was turned down.

"Turn him out in one of the paddocks and let's see him move," Ashleigh suggested.

"I bet he trots like an old plow horse," Tor joked.

Samantha shot him a look of mock annoyance. "You just wait, Tor. When you see his collection and stride, you'll want him for a jumper."

She led Chaser around the barn, the group following behind. Melanie and Christina hurried to the closest pasture and sat on the top fence board. When Samantha unhooked the lead line, Chaser strolled off, snuffling nosily at the ground.

"Hey, if he can't run, we can train him as a tracking dog," Tor teased.

"Oh, be quiet." Raising her arms, Samantha clucked and whooped. Chaser threw up his head, wheeled, and headed across the grass, bucking.

"Nope, we made a mistake. That there's a rodeo horse," Mike said in a fake drawl.

Chaser bucked and leaped happily. When he reached the end of the pasture, he slid to a stop, spun, and raced back in a flat-out gallop.

Melanie's eyes popped open. She wished she had a watch to clock him.

"What a stride!" Ashleigh exclaimed.

"He inherited that from his great-grandfather, Secretariat," Ian said proudly. He and Beth stood together, his arm around her shoulders.

"I'd better catch him before he breaks a leg," Samantha said. "Melanie, can you walk him awhile?"

When Melanie heard her name, she almost fell off the fence. "You want me to walk him?" she asked, glancing from Samantha to Ian. "Does that mean I can be his groom?"

Ian nodded once. "If you want the job."

"Do I!" Ecstatic, Melanie jumped down off the fence.

"Wait a minute, Dad," Kevin said. He'd been standing on the other side of Ian. "I thought you said I could be his groom."

"Sorry, son. I thought about it, but there's no way you can fit it into your schedule," Ian replied. "Basketball takes up too much of your time—you have practice after school almost every day and games on the weekends. Plus Mike's counting on you to help him break those yearlings."

Kevin's face turned white. Melanie stood frozen to the spot, with no idea what to say to him.

For a second Kevin just stared at his father's back. Then, without a word, he turned and walked away.

95

10

MELANIE RAN AFTER KEVIN. "HEY, I'M SORRY. BUT MAYBE your dad's right. You do practice every—"

Kevin stopped. Swinging around, he glared at her. "Knock it off, Melanie. You're not sorry at all. You got what you wanted. In fact, ever since you've been at Whitebrook, you've gotten everything you've wanted."

"That's not true," Melanie protested.

"Oh?" He cocked one brow. "Like what? Ashleigh, Mike, and your dad have bent over backward to grant your every wish. You wanted Pirate, you got Pirate. You wanted camp, you got camp. You wanted lessons on Trib, you got lessons on Trib. You didn't want to live in New York—"

"I get the picture," Melanie said, cutting him off. "But I've worked hard, too."

Kevin made a disgusted noise in his throat. "Get serious," he retorted, and strode away.

Melanie let him go. She realized he was disappointed that he didn't get to be Chaser's groom, but she was sick of his stomping off without hearing her side of it.

"Mel?" Samantha called. She was standing outside the pasture gate, holding Chaser. "Ready to take him?"

"Yes." Melanie jogged back to the group. "Any instructions?" she asked as she took the lead.

"Handle him with care," Tor joked.

"As if he were precious gold," Beth added.

"Just ignore those two," Samantha said, laughing. "Walk him until he's cool, then turn him out in one of the smaller paddocks to graze." Smiling up at the big colt, she scratched under his forelock. "He won't have many more days of freedom. This week we'll start working him under saddle."

"Can I help?" Melanie asked hopefully.

"Sure. I'll start him, but once he begins trotting on the track, you can ride him. We want to keep as light a weight on his back as possible to keep his legs sound."

Melanie jumped up and down. "Yes!"

Everybody laughed. As Melanie led Chaser away, Christina ran up behind her.

"So what's Kevin's problem?" she asked. "He looked mad."

"He's mad because Ian said he couldn't be Chaser's groom," Melanie said, stroking the colt's neck as they walked. "And mad at me because I am."

"He must be feeling kind of left out. Sometimes I feel that way when I'm practicing eventing, and everybody else is at the track rooting for some racehorse."

"But Kevin is totally involved with the racehorses."

"I know. But I think it bothered him that his sister and dad didn't even ask his opinion about buying Chaser."

"Well, he should be excited that they finally got their own racehorse. And it wasn't his money, anyway."

"Yeah, but Kevin was hoping to go to a basketball clinic over vacation," Christina explained. "And his dad said he'd have to earn the money himself."

"Even so, that's between him and his dad. He doesn't have to be so mad at me," Melanie said. "And his dad did have a good reason for not picking Kevin. He has basketball practice every afternoon. When would he have time to work with Chaser?"

"I don't know." Christina shrugged. "Guys. Go figure. Hey, want to go for a trail ride later?"

Melanie shook her head. "I'd better not." She thought about Kevin's remark that she never worked hard at anything. She had been trying, but maybe she needed to work even harder if she wanted to be taken seriously. "Want to work out with me later?"

"Nah. No offense, but that was really boring. I'd rather get my exercise by riding." When they reached the mare and foal barn, Christina started toward it. "I'm going to go say hi to Sterling."

Melanie halted Chaser. "Hey," she called. "You guys aren't mad about my not going on the overnight ride, are you?"

"No," Christina called, turning to walk backward while she talked. "And I don't want to sound like a naggy old parent, but everything in your life doesn't have to revolve around racehorses, you know. You can have fun, and I think the ride's going to be a blast."

"Thanks for the advice, Mommy," Melanie joked.

"All right. Don't listen to your mother," Christina teased before disappearing into the barn.

Chaser pulled on the lead, trying to get his head down for a bite of grass.

"Bored?" Melanie pulled up his head, then checked his chest to see if he was cool. "Just one more lap and I'll turn you out. I'll put Pirate with you, so you'll have some company."

But after thinking about it for a second, Melanie decided that was a bad idea. If Pirate should kick Chaser, he could really injure the new colt. Melanie remembered Tor and Beth's advice to treat him with care. She knew they weren't really joking.

If she wanted to be trusted with Chaser, she was going to have to pay attention. "Come on." Clucking, she led him around the yard, then headed to one of the paddocks. After she turned him out, she leaned against the fence and watched him. Since he'd already gotten out his leaps and bucks, he grazed calmly.

Melanie's heart swelled with pride. He was so handsome! And from now on, she'd be a part of his future. She'd show everyone how responsible she could be.

She thought back to Christina's comment about how much fun they were going to have on the weekend ride. She should have replied that she was already having fun. To her, working with the racehorses was better than anything.

"Since only a handful of you did well on last week's test on the amendments, we're going to discuss each question one by one," Mr. Sykes said. Pacing back and forth in front of his desk, the civics teacher began to read them off. "Number one—"

Seated in the back of the classroom, Melanie shook her head, trying to stay awake. She'd gotten an F on the test, so she knew she should listen. And she really should care. But it was Friday morning, and she was so tired that no matter how hard she tried, she kept dozing off.

All week long she'd been up at five-thirty in the morning to jog and do her workout, then groom and gallop whatever horse Naomi or Nathan didn't gallop. Every afternoon and evening she'd ridden Trib, Pirate, and Old Hay Bales, plus helped Ian, Mike, and Ashleigh work with the two-year-olds. Her muscles were sore and her brain was exhausted.

"Melanie, can you answer question five?" Mr. Sykes asked.

Jerking upright, Melanie focused on the test in front

of her. She located question five, which, amazingly, she had gotten right.

"Uh, the answer is C. The right to bear arms means everybody should be able to defend themselves," Melanie said quickly.

"Correct. Now, class, many of you picked B as the answer; however . . ."

Melanie breathed a sigh of relief. Usually Mr. Sykes asked her only one question each class period. She was off the hook for the rest of the hour.

After civics, she made it through PE . . . barely. Her arm and abdominal muscles were so sore from sit-ups and push-ups, she almost died trying to shoot a basketball. At the other end of the gym, some of the eighth-grade boys were playing a half-court game.

Melanie watched Kevin dribble down the court, weaving around the opposition as if they weren't even there, then effortlessly make a layup. Every morning he'd been up early to ride Thunder, and he had practice every afternoon. She knew Kevin had always been an A student, too. How did he keep up with it all?

"Did you know that Kevin's going to be a starting forward for the JV team?" Katie said from beside Melanie.

"I know, and he's only in eighth grade."

"Yeah, but he's awesome. He's been playing ever since I've known him."

"I bet some of the ninth and tenth graders aren't too happy about his starting."

Katie shrugged. "If the team wins, who cares? It's not like he's a ball hog or a show-off like some of the players. He's just good." She nudged Melanie in the side. "Too bad you're not coming on the ride with us next weekend. Most girls would be dying to spend time with the big sports star."

"Give me a break," Melanie groaned. "Besides, Kevin and I aren't exactly a couple."

"I know. But you're always together."

"Not lately."

"Really? Then is it all right if I tell Heather he's available?" Kate pointed toward a willowy blonde who looked good even in her baggy gym shorts. "She's liked him forever."

Melanie studied Heather. She had gorgeous blue eyes and long blond hair, and she was tall enough to snag the rebound and make a perfect jump shot.

"Sure. I don't care," Melanie muttered.

"Good!" Katie exclaimed, immediately running over to Heather.

Melanie wanted to kick herself. Why had she told Katie that she didn't care about Kevin? She did care. But it was obvious that he didn't care about her.

When the gym teacher blew the whistle, Melanie dragged herself into the locker room. She wasn't sweaty but she showered, letting the warm water beat against her sore muscles. Maybe it would help keep her awake for her afternoon classes.

After PE, Christina met her in the doorway of the

cafeteria. "Is it true?" she exclaimed. "Have you and Kevin broken up?"

Melanie gave her a puzzled look. "We were never going out."

"You weren't officially going out, but you were together a lot, and that's the same thing."

"No, it's not." Melanie went over to a lunch table and tossed her paper bag onto it. "We're friends. At least we were." Still tired, she flopped onto the bench. She opened her bag and pulled out half a turkey sandwich and a boxed juice.

"You'd better start eating more," Christina said. "Yesterday all you had was yogurt."

With a shrug, Melanie bit into her sandwich. "I need to keep my weight down if I'm going to ride Chaser."

"Chaser, Chaser, Chaser," Christina grumbled. "That's all I've heard the last few days."

"Sterling, Sterling, Sterling," Melanie repeated. "That's all I've heard for the last few months."

Laughing, Christina dumped out her lunch box. A bag of chocolate chip cookies slid in front of Melanie. Her mouth started to water. "I made them last night," Christina said. "While you were racing Old Hay Bales. By the way, did you win?"

"No," Melanie replied. "But I did manage to stay balanced for a couple of minutes."

Just then Katie slid into the seat across from Melanie and Christina. "Heather is so psyched," she said. "She's going to call Kevin tonight."

Melanie bit into her sandwich, trying to act uninterested.

"So, are you ready for the big ride?" Katie asked Christina, changing the subject.

"Yeah, I can't wait," Christina answered. "Sam and Tor are excited, too, even though they have a ton of work to do around their farm. I think they need the break."

When the bell rang, Melanie was glad to get away. She was sick of hearing about the trail ride.

Her afternoon classes moved as slowly as snails. Melanie took a short nap in science. Finally English, her last-period class, rolled around. As usual, Ms. Hanlon assigned too much homework.

Only five minutes more, Melanie thought, her gaze glued to the clock. Already she could feel her energy returning. This afternoon Samantha was coming to work with Chaser, and Melanie was going to help her. She couldn't wait.

"I'm passing out midterm progress reports," Miss Hanlon announced as she went up and down the rows of desks. "These are for all subjects. Your parent or guardian must sign them. They are due back Monday morning in homeroom."

As she passed by Melanie, Miss Hanlon dropped a folded white slip on her desk. Melanie stared at it. She knew her grades weren't going to be too hot this time around. She'd barely studied, and many nights she hadn't gotten around to finishing her homework. Still, she was smart and she was used to a tough private school. She couldn't have done too horribly.

Hesitantly Melanie reached out and slid the white sheet toward her. When she opened it, her eyes widened in horror. English: F. Civics: F. She couldn't believe it. She was flunking two subjects.

Mounting fear rose in her throat. She couldn't tell her dad about her grades. He'd be so mad, he'd probably forbid her to ride during the school week. And she couldn't tell Ashleigh and Mike, either. They'd tell her dad, and her career as a jockey would be over before it started.

Refolding the grade slip, Melanie slid it into the back pocket of her jeans. She couldn't tell anyone, even if she had to lie. There was no way she was giving up a minute of her time with the horses.

11

"SO WHAT DID YOU GET ON YOUR PROGRESS REPORT?" Christina asked as they walked up Whitebrook's lane.

"Okay grades. Nothing spectacular," Melanie fibbed. She'd spent so much time practicing what she was going to say to Christina that the lie rolled smoothly from her mouth. "My dad won't be too pleased, but then, he wants me to get straight A's. What did you get?"

"Three A's and two B's."

Melanie grimaced. She should have guessed her cousin would do well, which made it even worse. Ashleigh and Mike would probably expect her grades to be as good as Christina's. "That's great," she said, trying to sound enthusiastic.

"Let me see what you got."

Melanie shook her head. "The slip's in my pack, and

I've got to hurry. Sam's going to be here to work with Chaser," she added, hoping her cousin would drop the subject.

"That's right." Christina started to walk faster. "I want to watch, too. Pretty soon she's going to start Sweet Dreams under saddle, and she wants me to help."

The two girls hurried up the drive to the house. A note was on the back door from Ashleigh saying she and Mike had gone to the hardware store, and there were bagels for a snack.

Melanie exhaled in relief. Thank goodness they were gone. As soon as Christina showed her parents her progress report, they'd be asking Melanie about hers. She needed to figure out a convincing story.

Christina plunked her pack on the kitchen table and began to rummage in the refrigerator. "Want cream cheese on your bagel?"

"None for me, thanks."

Straightening, Christina pulled out the milk and cream cheese. "Melanie, you eat like a mouse. You need food for energy if you're going to keep up your crazy exercise schedule."

"I feel great," Melanie called, already on her way down the hall. Taking the steps two at a time, she went into her room and changed into her barn jeans. She didn't have time to eat. Samantha would be there any minute. Besides, she was too excited. She was dying to find out what Chaser would do when

Samantha got on him for the first time.

When Melanie went back into the kitchen, Christina had half a bagel in one hand and a glass of orange juice in the other. "I'm eating a half for you," she told Melanie, her mouth full.

Melanie laughed. "See you at the barn, then."

Samantha's small pickup was already parked by the training barn. When Melanie went in, Chaser was in crossties and Sam was picking out his feet.

"Hi!" Melanie called, and at the sight of the handsome colt, all her worries about grades disappeared.

"Good afternoon, gorgeous," she crooned as she scratched his forelock and ears. Ducking his head, he wiggled his nose in delight. "How's Mellie's wittle boy?"

With a groan, Samantha set down his hoof and straightened. "Don't tell me you're going to talk baby talk to him—you'll ruin him," she joked.

"I can't help it. He's sooo cu-ute!" Melanie laughed. "What can I do to help?"

"I'll show you what bridle he's going to be using: a full cheek snaffle with a fat bit. He's got a soft mouth. We want to keep it that way."

"Your friend got him used to the saddle and stuff already?" Melanie asked as she followed Samantha into the tack room.

"Yes. She's had him on a longe line and worked him lightly in a round pen. He's going to be one easy colt to break." She gave Melanie a serious look. "He's also

108

been treated with kindness and respect. We're going to continue in the same way."

Melanie nodded. She knew that most good trainers worked slowly and gently with the young horses. But she also had heard stories about trainers who pushed their yearlings, using abrupt, rushed methods because they wanted fast results.

In silence, the two tacked Chaser up. He stood quietly, accepting the bit without hesitation, though Melanie had to stand on tiptoe to slip the crown piece over his ears. She put the halter back over the bridle and clipped a lead line to the ring. When Chaser was ready, Ian came into the barn followed by Christina, who'd changed into her riding clothes.

Ian's face brightened when he saw the colt. "How's my investment today, ladies?"

"*Our* investment," Samantha corrected before going into the tack room, "is ready for his first rider."

Ian nodded. "Melanie, you've got control of his head. I'll partner Samantha and make sure she's safe."

"Is it okay if I watch?" Christina asked.

"Sure, but stay in the doorway of the tack room. That way, if he does explode, you can duck inside and he won't crash into you."

"He's not going to explode," Melanie protested. "He's a pussycat."

Ian cocked one bushy brow. "Ever see a cat when it's fighting mad?"

"I think Melanie's right," Samantha said as she

came out of the tack room carrying her helmet. She'd already donned her chaps. "He's accepted everything calmly so far."

"All right. Obviously you both have far more experience than I, the person who's been working with colts since . . ." Gazing skyward, Ian silently counted off on his fingers.

"All right, Dad, we understand what you're saying," Samantha said with a laugh. Coming over to Chaser, she checked his girth, then gave him a pat. "Dad will give me a leg up," she told Melanie. "First I'll belly him to see how he accepts my weight."

Melanie nodded. She knew that meant that Sam would lie across the saddle, her legs dangling on the left side. If Chaser did jump, she could easily slide off. Also, Ian would be right beside her, ready to catch her if she fell.

"Your job is to keep him from getting excited," Ian added.

"Right," Melanie said, though she was feeling nervous. Chaser was probably nine hundred pounds. She weighed less than a hundred. If he did explode, it would be no contest.

Ian gave Samantha a leg up. She sprang up lightly, but instead of throwing her right leg over the saddle, she lay across it. Ian stood right beside her, his hand on her left leg.

Chaser raised his head as if surprised. "That's a

good boy," Melanie crooned, her grasp tight on the lead close to the halter ring.

Samantha slid off, patted Chaser, then did it again. This time Melanie could feel the muscles in Chaser's neck bunch, and his eyes rolled back, so she could see the whites.

"Sam, I'd bail out if I were you," Melanie said, keeping her voice calm.

Instantly Samantha slid off, the same second Chaser erupted. Twisting sideways, he kicked out, striking the wall with his right hind leg. Ian and Samantha scrambled for safety, jumping into the tack room doorway.

Pulling Chaser's head into her chest, Melanie turned him in a quick circle. She knew there was no way she could hold him if he wanted to take off, and a tight circle was the best way to keep him moving but under her control.

Her heart was beating a mile a minute, and her adrenaline was pumping. *Stay calm so you can keep him calm,* she told herself.

She took a deep breath. About the third time around, Chaser lowered his head and let out a sigh, and she could feel his muscles relax. Melanie's shoulders slumped in relief.

"Whoa." She halted him in front of the tack room door. Samantha, Ian, and Christina were peeking out cautiously.

"All clear?" Ian said.

Melanie nodded. Tears pricked her eyes. "I'm so sorry," she blurted.

"About what?" Samantha asked, taking the lead from Melanie.

"He never should have done that! I should have had him under control."

Ian shook his head. "You did great. In fact, you saved Sam from being tossed ten feet in the air."

"I did?" Melanie blinked.

"Sure. By warning her. How'd you know he was going to blow up?"

"His body language. I wasn't sure. . . ." Melanie sniffed and wiped off her cheeks. "But Trib gets the same look when he's about to pull something stupid."

Christina laughed. "Maybe every jockey wanna-be should start with Trib."

Samantha patted Melanie on the back. "You did good, Mel. And look." She gestured to Chaser, who stood dead quiet, as if he'd never blown up. "You kept your head, so he kept his. If you'd gotten mad or let him get away, it would have been an awful situation."

"Right. Ready to belly him again?" Ian asked his daughter.

Melanie's eyes widened. "You're doing it again? You're not afraid?"

Samantha laughed. "Oh, that was nothing. You were right. Chaser is a pussycat. From now on, he'll be a piece of cake."

112

•••

Saturday Melanie woke early. Ian was putting her on Pride's Perfection that morning. She'd ponied him all week and his leg had stayed cool with no swelling. Ian had decided a trot around the track would do Perfection good.

For a second she lay in bed, thinking back to her fall off the colt. It hadn't been anybody's fault. Perfection had stumbled, but being thrown off a tall, swiftly moving Thoroughbred had really terrified Melanie.

Automatically she touched her cheek. Her only injuries had been some scrapes, an ugly bruise, and some very sore muscles, but it had taken her a while to get back on another racehorse. Would the fear come back when she got on Perfection?

Throwing off the blanket, Melanie scowled. *You're only trotting him, stupid,* she told herself. Besides, if she was going to be a jockey, she'd better get over her fear. Falling and injuries were part of the job.

When she went downstairs, Ashleigh was drinking coffee while reading the newspaper. "Taking it easy this morning?" Melanie asked.

Ashleigh nodded. "Mike's doing rounds this morning. I made some apple-cinnamon muffins." She waved toward a basket on the counter.

"Yum." Melanie grabbed one. She took a big bite. *I'll eat only one,* she told herself. "Delicious. I don't know how you have time to bake."

113

Ashleigh laughed. "Gee, haven't you noticed all the frozen dinners I serve? Hey, I hear Ian's putting you on Perfection."

"Yeah. I'm excited, and a little nervous," she admitted.

"Good. Then you'll stay on your toes, though both Ian and Sam have been very complimentary about your work with Chaser. And it's hard to get a compliment out of Ian."

Melanie couldn't help but smile. Opening the refrigerator door, she poured a small glass of milk and took a drink.

Ashleigh put down the newspaper. "By the way, Christina showed me her progress report. Did you get yours as well?"

Melanie was so startled by the question, she choked on the gulp of milk.

Jumping up, Ashleigh pounded her on the back. "Okay?"

Melanie nodded. "Yes," she gasped. "Just went down the wrong pipe." She took a couple of ragged breaths, then glanced at Ashleigh, hoping her aunt had forgotten her question.

"Progress report?" Ashleigh repeated, looking at her with an expectant expression.

"In my backpack," Melanie said. "I'll show you tonight."

"Good. You can call your dad then, too. I'm sure he's going to want to know how well you're doing. Your

114

first report card was just okay. I know he was hoping you'd pull up your grades this marking period."

"Right." Melanie finished off the milk and, taking the muffin with her, headed for the door. "Ian's expecting me."

When she went outside, she exhaled in relief. But her relief didn't last long. How long could she keep the truth from Ashleigh, Mike, and her dad?

Fear stabbed her insides, and her stomach rolled. Feeling nauseous, she tossed the last bite of muffin into a bush.

Get hold of yourself, Melanie Graham, she told herself firmly. She'd tell Ashleigh and her dad that she'd lost her progress report. If she worked hard, she could pull the two F's up before the end of the marking period.

Melanie lengthened her stride as she hurried to the barn. She'd made a plan. Everything would be fine.

So why didn't she feel any better?

12

"A QUIET TROT AROUND THE TRACK," IAN TOLD MELANIE AS she began working Perfection that afternoon. The feisty colt chewed his bit, eager to go. "I'll walk with you to the oval."

"Thanks." Since she was just trotting, Melanie had left her stirrups fairly long so that her seat would be more secure. She hoped Ian didn't notice. He might take it as a sign she was afraid.

Was she? Melanie bit her lip, not sure of the answer. Perfection was definitely a handful, but no worse than most of the colts who raced. As Maureen had told her, she needed to learn how to control the horses she rode, not by force, but by reading their body language and knowing how to react.

She'd learned to read Heart of Stone. She could do the same with Perfection.

"Kevin's through galloping Thunder, so you'll be alone, no distractions." Ian patted the colt's neck as they walked. He grinned up at Melanie. "You'll do fine," he said, as if he understood her nervousness.

"Right." Melanie hoped she sounded convincing. When they reached the gap in the railing, Kevin and Thunder were just coming out. The five-year-old looked shiny and racing-fit.

Jealousy and a touch of fear filled Melanie. Kevin had done a terrific job with Thunder. If they found out about Melanie's miserable grades, Ian and Samantha would surely let Kevin take over as Chaser's groom.

"Thunder looks good," Melanie said, swallowing her feelings.

Ian nodded. "Yup, he looks ready to race again."

"This old guy could beat any youngster on the farm," Kevin called, and glanced from his dad to Melanie. "Including that hotshot Perfection."

Melanie bristled. Even though she was feeling upset, she'd tried to compliment Kevin. Why had he jumped on her and his dad like that?

"Mike's entering him in a Thanksgiving weekend race," Kevin added. "And I bet he'll win."

"Great." Melanie didn't know what else to say since every word out of her mouth seemed to make Kevin mad.

"Ready?" Ian asked Melanie, as if he hadn't even heard Kevin.

When she nodded, he added, "Keep your attention on your horse."

Melanie steered Perfection through the gap and onto the smooth surface of the oval. Since several horses had worked already, the dirt was streaked with trails of prints.

Perfection broke into a jog. Taking a deep breath, Melanie pulled him to a walk. She was determined to be the driver.

The colt slowed, but she could feel his muscles tense in eagerness. The ponying had helped to build him up again, so he was ready for action. Melanie squeezed him lightly with her heels, and he leaped into a rough trot that threw her forward.

"Easy," she crooned. Her mind went back to her dressage lessons. Half-halts—Mona had made her practice them until Melanie had nightmares about them.

But she realized that just like in dressage, she needed to use her body and aids to balance and slow Perfection, yet keep his energy moving forward. Deepening her seat, she wiggled her fingers on the reins, asking him to give to the bit. Slowly Melanie felt the colt collect beneath her. His stride became longer and smoother.

The chilly morning air brushed against her cheeks, and as Perfection trotted around the track Melanie's lips tilted into a smile. This was definitely heaven.

"Only once around, buddy," Melanie said when

they reached the gap in what seemed like no time at all. The colt responded to her signal and walked, though he was ready for more.

Still on the rail, Ian gave her a thumbs-up. "Walk him once around, then bring him in," he called. "That was a good start. Monday we'll do the same, then start increasing the distance. By the end of the week, you should be able to canter him."

All right! Melanie grinned. She'd made it. The rest of the week would be easy.

After cooling Perfection, she galloped First Term, a colt out of Terminator, one of Whitebrook's stallions. Terminator had a nasty disposition, and so did this colt. Fortunately, his groom, Mark Anderson, knew how to handle him. If Melanie could avoid his teeth while mounting, he was great to ride.

When she was finished, she ponied two young colts on Pirate, then helped Ian and Maureen work with Sly Miss, one of the coming two-year-olds. She was a petite filly out of Miss America. Melanie liked working with her since she was sensible and quiet, more like a seasoned gelding than a capricious filly.

"Ready to get on her again today?" Maureen asked.

Melanie nodded. She still wore her helmet and chaps.

"We'll belly her once," Ian said. "If she's quiet, I'll boost you into the saddle."

While Maureen held the filly, Ian gave Melanie a leg

up. For a minute she lay sprawled over the small training saddle. The blood rushed to her head, and she suddenly felt like fainting.

Melanie slid off. Her head was swimming. She fell against Ian, who fortunately caught her.

"Are you all right?" he asked.

She gave him a weak smile. "Fine. I didn't eat much breakfast today. I guess it's catching up to me."

"What about lunch?" Maureen asked.

"Lunch?" Stepping away from Ian, Melanie leaned against the wall, trying to clear her head.

"It's after twelve," Maureen said.

"Oh. I didn't realize it was so late." Melanie waited a minute, then straightened. "Okay, I'm ready to get on her."

"Not so fast, young lady," Ian said. "Make sure you're good and steady."

"I'm fine!" Melanie insisted. Even though her legs still felt a little wobbly, there was no way she was going to admit it—especially to Ian.

When they were finished, Melanie started back to the house to get some lunch. It had been stupid to eat only half a muffin for breakfast. Jockeys had to keep their weight down, but they had to keep their strength up, too.

Christina was sitting at the kitchen table with Katie, going over a list.

"Hi," Melanie said as she headed over to the sink to wash her hands. "What're you guys doing?"

"Making sure we have everything we need for next weekend," Katie said. "The camp isn't near any stores, and we'd hate to get there and find out we didn't have soap."

"Or toilet paper," Christina added. She looked up from the list. "What's wrong with you?"

Melanie stopped scrubbing. "What do you mean?"

"You're white as a ghost."

"Just hungry. Did you guys eat?"

"Yup. There's tuna salad already made in a bowl."

Just the thought of all that mayonnaise made Melanie's stomach churn. "I think I'll have a salad."

"Are you on a diet or something?" Katie asked.

"No. Why?"

"'Cause you're starting to look like one of those waiflike models in the fashion magazines."

"Gee, thanks for the compliment," Melanie muttered.

"Did you hear about Heather and Kevin?" Katie asked.

Grabbing a dish towel, Melanie turned around. "Hear what?"

"He asked her out."

Totally surprised, Melanie stopped drying her hands. Christina was staring at her, waiting to see how Melanie was going to react.

"That's nice," Melanie said. Dropping the towel on the counter, she turned and headed back outside. Suddenly she wasn't hungry.

She hurried across the yard and up the drive. Tears stung her eyes. *I'm not mad,* she told herself. *I'm not even sad.*

So what was she, then?

Confused. She and Kevin had been such good friends. When she'd first come to Whitebrook and everything had been so different, he'd really been there for her. Now they were strangers. No, worse than strangers. Kevin acted as if he hated her, and she had no idea why.

She knew she should ask him what was wrong. But they hardly saw each other these days, and when she did see him, he was so mean that she hated to talk to him.

When she reached the barn, she headed for the paddock at the back where Pirate was turned out. Even though she'd been riding and working with dozens of horses, he was still her favorite—they had a special bond. Like Kevin, he'd helped her when she first arrived from New York and was feeling pretty blue.

"Hey, buddy." As soon as Pirate heard her, he came over to the fence. She leaned her arms on the top board. Ducking his head, he snuffled her hands, then her face.

"Sorry, no treat today." Sighing, Melanie propped her chin on her hands. She didn't know why she felt so depressed. She was doing a great job with Chaser, Perfection, and the young horses. Hadn't she gotten lots of praise from everybody?

She was on her way to proving she had what it took

to become a jockey, Melanie told herself. Grades, guys, friends, trail rides—they'd just have to wait.

"I can't find my grade slip anywhere," Melanie told her aunt and uncle Sunday night. The family was seated around the dining room table having a rare sit-down dinner together. Ashleigh had baked a ham and Mike had made his special sweet potato casserole. Everything had tasted delicious until Ashleigh mentioned grades.

"It must have fallen out of my backpack," Melanie added. Seated across the table, Christina gave her a strange look.

"At least call your dad tonight and tell him what your grades were," Mike said.

"I would, but I didn't look at the slip that carefully, so I don't know my grades," Melanie said, adding to the lie.

Christina's brows shot up and she gave Melanie a look that said, *They're never going to believe that one.* Melanie hoped her cousin would keep her mouth shut.

"Well, first thing tomorrow morning, you'd better go to your counselor and get another copy," Ashleigh said. "It's supposed to be signed."

"Right. May I have the rolls, please?" she asked, hoping everybody would forget about grades.

Mike passed them to her, and Christina launched into the plans for the weekend trail ride. Melanie let out

123

her breath. Saved—until the next day. Then what was she going to do?

"Melanie, why aren't you going on the ride?" Ashleigh asked. "It sounds like fun."

"Uh, I'd rather stay at Whitebrook. There's so much to do."

"You can take some time off to be with your friends," Mike said as he buttered another roll.

"But I *am* with friends," Melanie explained. "I love being around Naomi and Sam and everyone."

"Gee, thanks," Christina huffed. "I guess we just don't count anymore."

Melanie frowned and put down her fork. "That's not what I mean, Chris. I'd just rather hang around here."

"Whatever." Christina shrugged, but Melanie could tell she was a little miffed.

"Well, I think you're making a mistake," Ashleigh said. "You're only thirteen. This is the age when you should be hanging out with friends and having fun."

"Not if I want to be a jockey in three years," Melanie said. "Besides, Aunt Ashleigh, weren't you just like me when you were my age?"

"Well—" Ashleigh grinned sheepishly.

Later that night, Christina came into her room. Melanie was trying to read *Romeo and Juliet* for English, but she kept falling asleep.

"Wake up, Mel." Christina plopped on her bed, making the springs squeak.

124

"I'm awake," Melanie mumbled, pulling the book off her face.

"So why'd you lie to my parents about the report card?" she asked. "Are you in major-league trouble?"

Melanie nodded. "Yes," she admitted.

"What did you get?"

"Two F's."

Christina's jaw dropped.

"You don't have to act so surprised," Melanie said. "Haven't you ever gotten an F?"

Christina shook her head. "Never. Not even a D. And not many C's, either."

"Oh, great." Melanie groaned and plopped the book back on her face. "I'm doomed. Your mom and dad will be totally shocked. At least my dad's used to lousy grades."

"What are you going to do?" Christina asked, sounding more worried than Melanie.

"I don't know what to do. I mean, I really do think I can pull the F's to C's by the end of the semester."

"By falling asleep in the middle of studying?" Christina joked.

"I'll just have to work harder. And I'd really appreciate it if you would help me," she said.

"I'll be happy to study with you, but I can't take the tests for you, you know. And tomorrow you're going to have to show them the grade slip. Unless you do something really devious, like forge their signatures."

Melanie whipped the book off her face. "What a great idea!"

Christina held up her hands, shaking her head. "I was just kidding, Mel."

"I know." Melanie knew she was trapped. The next day after school, she'd have to face Ashleigh and Mike. "I'm just afraid they'll keep me from riding."

"Yuck." Christina wrinkled her nose. "I can't imagine not being allowed to ride Sterling. That would be the worst ever."

Melanie had to agree.

13

MONDAY AFTERNOON MELANIE DRAGGED HERSELF UP THE driveway. Christina hadn't come home on the bus. Katie's mom was picking up the two girls at school and taking them to the tack shop to buy warm gear for the weekend.

Melanie was going to have to face Ashleigh alone.

Her "missing" progress report was in her backpack. The whole ride home, she'd racked her brains trying to come up with some way to keep her aunt and uncle from finding out about her grades. The night before, in a flurry of desperation, she'd even called her old friend, Aynslee, in New York. But Aynslee had advised Melanie to come clean before she was in even bigger trouble.

A cold gust of wind chilled Melanie to the bone. Or was it the thought of Mike and Ashleigh's wrath? Not to mention her father's. He'd agreed to let her stay at

Whitebrook after she'd convinced him she would be happier and not get in as much trouble. Well, she was happier, all right, but as far as her dad was concerned, failing two classes was the worst kind of trouble.

She stopped on the front porch of the house, finally forcing herself to go inside. Fortunately, it was quiet, so she knew everyone must be at the barns. She changed, grabbed an apple, then hurried up the drive to get it over with.

The sight of the veterinarian's truck in front of the training barn made her break into a jog. When she raced inside, she spotted Mike and Ashleigh. Her heart sank to her knees when she realized they were in front of Chaser's stall.

"What's wrong?" she called as she ran toward them.

"Take it easy," Ashleigh said, slipping an arm around Melanie's shoulder when she stopped next to her. "A slight touch of colic."

"Will he be all right? Was it my fault?" She blurted the last sentence.

Ashleigh gave her a surprised look. "No. We'd been increasing his feed since he got here, and it was just too much rich food. Dr. Lanum says we'll have to back him off for a while."

"Oh." Melanie's shoulders sagged. "Can I see him?"

Mike grinned. "He's not exactly in the best of humor," he said, stepping aside.

Melanie peered in. Samantha stood in the stall holding Chaser, who had a tube down one nostril. Dr.

Lanum was funneling medicine through the tube and into his throat.

Chaser looked as miserable as Melanie felt. "Does Ian know?" Ian had left early that morning to deliver two horses they'd been training to another farm.

"Yes, Mike called him on his cell phone," Ashleigh assured her. "Everything's under control."

"I should have been here instead of stupid school," Melanie muttered under her breath.

She watched as Dr. Lanum gently pulled the tube from Chaser's nostril. The colt shook his head, then rubbed his muzzle against the stall wall. Stepping inside, Melanie massaged his nose. "That felt terrible, didn't it?"

Samantha handed her the lead line. "Do you have time to walk him?"

"Of course."

"The medicine should relieve the cramps and speed the manure through his intestines," Dr. Lanum said as she packed up her things. "Since it's spasmodic colic, which is like a stomachache, you can feed him a little hay tonight. Turn him out tomorrow, and by Wednesday he should be ready for light work."

"Great. While you're here, can you take a look at one of the broodmares?" Ashleigh asked.

The three left. Samantha watched Melanie lead Chaser from the stall and down the aisle. "He seems better already," she said. "When Dr. L. put the tube into his stomach, it relieved some of the gas pressure."

"Who noticed Chaser wasn't right?" Melanie asked when she turned the colt and walked back toward Samantha.

"Jonnie. Chaser didn't clean up his feed this morning. Jonnie turned him out, and when he checked on him later, Chaser looked agitated. Jonnie phoned me immediately, then told Mike. By the time I got here, Chaser was pawing the ground. It looked like colic, so we called Dr. L. and walked him till she came."

"Thank goodness he was all right."

"You're telling me." Samantha ran her fingers through her hair in a gesture of exhaustion. "Can you handle him from here? I've got to go back to Whisperwood to teach a lesson, then feed my own horses. Tor's teaching a clinic and won't be back until tomorrow."

"Go." Melanie waved her away. When Samantha left, the barn was quiet except for an occasional snort. Chaser walked listlessly down the aisle beside Melanie. She could hear his stomach gurgle, a good sign. She knew mild colic happened to a lot of young horses when their feed was changed, and it usually wasn't life-threatening. Still, just seeing Dr. Lanum had scared her.

Twenty minutes later Mike came into the barn to check on them. "How's the sick boy doing?"

"Better," Melanie said.

"Spoken like a proud mother." Mike felt Chaser's belly. "His muscles feel more relaxed. Go ahead and put him back in his stall. Maureen could use your help in the mare and foal barn. Since Jonnie left and

130

Ian isn't here, we're a little shorthanded."

"I'll be glad to help." Melanie headed for Chaser's stall. "Should I keep checking on him?"

"I'll keep my eye on him," Mike assured her.

Melanie led Chaser into his stall. When she unhooked the lead line, he walked over to the corner and, after heaving a sigh, lowered his head as if he needed to rest.

"Hang in there, guy," Melanie whispered. She closed the door, hung up the lead line, then hurried to the mare and foal barn. She wondered what Maureen was doing. Maybe feeding, since Jonnie wasn't there.

When she got to the barn, she didn't see anyone. "Maureen?" she called.

"Down here!"

Melanie headed toward the sound of the assistant trainer's voice. Finally she spotted her in one of the weanlings' stalls. "What's up?" Melanie asked. "Mike said you needed help."

"What I need is five arms," Maureen said, laughing. She was holding a towel in one hand and the cheek-piece of the foal's halter with the other. Melanie recognized Missy, the gray foal Christina had worked with over the summer.

Maureen laid the towel over Missy's neck. The foal turned in a circle, trying to get away from the feel of it. Gently Maureen slid it off.

Melanie knew this was one way to prepare a foal for eventually accepting a blanket and saddle. Opening the stall door, she stepped inside. "I'll hold her."

"Thanks. Usually Kevin does this with me, but he had practice today." Maureen said. "He's really good with the foals."

When she heard Kevin's name, Melanie's stomach lurched.

"Most of the foals I can handle myself, but Missy's been a pickle since day one," Maureen continued.

Melanie chuckled. "Christina had a hard time with her, too."

"If she doesn't settle down, I'm going to suggest that Mike sell her."

"Why?" Melanie scratched Missy's fuzzy mane. "Doesn't it show she's got spunk enough to win a race?"

Maureen shrugged. "It takes more than spunk. It takes brains and some common sense. When you're on top of a horse galloping forty miles an hour with ten other horses and jockeys crowding around you, all heading for the same sweet spot on the rail, you and your horse have got to trust each other." She nodded at Missy. "After all this time, Missy's as mistrustful as a deer."

Melanie eyed the filly. Did Missy realize her fate was being decided?

Melanie helped Maureen with four other weanlings and then went back to check on Chaser. He was contentedly munching hay.

"Feeling better?" she asked, carrying a grooming box into his stall. When the colt looked at her with his big brown eyes, she melted. She couldn't stand to have anything happen to him.

Melanie was brushing out Chaser's tail with long, methodical strokes of the stiff brush when Ashleigh came to the stall door. "Melanie, I need to talk to you a minute."

From the concerned tone in her aunt's voice, Melanie knew something was wrong. Had she forgotten to put something away? Had one of the weanlings gotten loose?

"What's wrong?" Melanie dropped the brush in the box and opened the stall door. Ashleigh motioned for her to come out into the aisle.

"I just got a call from Ms. Price, your school counselor," Ashleigh said.

Melanie grimaced. She'd forgotten all about her report card.

"She wanted to know why you didn't return your signed report card."

Melanie couldn't think of what to say.

"I told her you lost yours and were supposed to get another copy from her today. She said you hadn't been in," Ashleigh continued.

"I found it at school. I was going to show it to you this afternoon, but when I saw Chaser I forgot."

"I'm glad to hear that, but I already asked her what your grades were."

"And she told you?" Melanie squeaked.

Ashleigh nodded. "No wonder you 'lost' your progress report Friday. I would have made mine disappear, too, if I had gotten two F's."

133

Melanie gulped.

4elanie, that's failing, flunking," Ashleigh declared. "Too many F's, and you'll have to repeat eighth grade."

"I'll pull them up, really," Melanie said.

Crossing her arms in front of her chest, Ashleigh began to pace up and down the aisle. "What is your father going to say? He's going to wonder what I've been doing as your guardian, which is a good question. What *have* I been doing?" Halting in front of Melanie, she directed the question at her.

Before Melanie could even open her mouth, her aunt went on, "Nothing. I never checked your homework or made sure you studied. I never even looked at your papers or asked about test grades. I just assumed you were as responsible as Christina."

Melanie grimaced when she heard Christina's name.

"I was so happy to have you helping with the horses," Ashleigh went on, "and so excited about your interest in the farm that I forgot your school responsibilities are just as important. More important."

Melanie felt panic rising in her chest. Was this where Ashleigh told her she was going to restrict her riding?

"I'll do better, Aunt Ashleigh, really," Melanie blurted. "I'll learn how to manage my time so I'll get all my homework done."

"It's not just homework. You need a life, Melanie, other than the farm. When you first came here, you really had fun with Christina's friends. What happened?"

"I'd rather work with the horses," Melanie said.

"That's great. But you also need to balance it out with other things. Like Kevin and Christina do."

"I'm sorry," Melanie said finally. And she was. "But I thought at least you'd understand about wanting to be with the horses more than anything."

"I do." Ashleigh let out a big sigh. "And I bet I sounded just like my mother used to. Which isn't all bad. I know you want to be a jockey, Melanie, and it does take hard work. But most jockeys' careers don't last long. They get too big or get injured. They need something to fall back on."

"Then I'll become a trainer like you!" Melanie protested.

Ashleigh frowned. "You know what I'm saying."

Melanie hung her head. "So what's next?" she asked hesitantly.

"That's up to your father."

Melanie groaned. "Do you have to tell him?" she pleaded. "Can't you wait until the next report period? By then I will have brought up my grades. I promise."

Ashleigh shook her head. "I'm not telling him. You are. Tonight. And whatever punishment he decides on, Mike and I will carry out. Is that understood?"

Melanie nodded. She understood all right. After that night, her life would be over.

14

MELANIE HELD THE RECEIVER OF THE PHONE AWAY FROM HER
ear. Her father always blew up when it came to grades,
so she was used to his reaction. When she'd lived with
him in New York, she'd managed to smooth things over
a little by putting on her contrite-and-adorable act.
Hugs and tears had helped, too—none of which was
easy to pull off over the phone.

"Are you through yelling?" she finally asked when
no more shouting came over the line. She was sitting
tensely on the sofa in the family room. Christina and
Ashleigh were next door in the kitchen. Melanie knew
they had to be listening.

"Put Ashleigh on the phone," her father said tersely.
"I want to hear her explanation of what happened.
Then I want to talk to you again."

"Yes, sir," Melanie said, figuring the "sir" was a nice

touch. "But don't blame her," she added quickly.

"I don't," her father stated. "You are thirteen and quite capable of messing up on your own."

No kidding. Melanie held back a sigh.

"Ashleigh," Melanie called into the kitchen. "A very mad father wants to talk to you."

A second later Ashleigh came into the family room, Christina tagging behind her. Melanie handed her aunt the phone.

"What did he say?" Christina whispered.

Melanie stood up, linked arms with her cousin, and pulled her into the kitchen. "He said it was all your fault."

"My fault!" Christina exclaimed.

Melanie burst into giggles.

Christina gave her an annoyed look. "How can you joke at a time like this?"

"Oh, I don't know." Suddenly depressed, Melanie plunked herself down in a kitchen chair. "Because it's out of my control. Besides, I've had lots of practice dealing with irate parents. It's no use getting all weepy and sad—unless, of course, it serves a purpose, like making them feel sorry for you."

Christina punched Melanie on the arm. "You are so rotten."

"Not rotten. Desperate." Melanie grabbed her cousin's wrist. "I'll just die if they don't let me work with the horses."

"I know what you mean." Christina slumped in the opposite chair. "I would, too."

For a little while they sat in miserable silence. Melanie tried to hear what Ashleigh was saying, but gave up. "So what'd you get at the tack shop for the big weekend trail ride?" she finally asked Christina, hoping to take her mind off her problems.

"Gloves, ear warmers, and riding sweats. Mona said it'll be really chilly in the mountains. By the way, Kevin's going on the ride, too."

"Why did he change his mind?"

Christina shrugged. "Why don't you ask him yourself?"

"Like he'd tell me the answer," Melanie grumbled.

"You two still aren't speaking?"

"Oh, we speak. He growls at me and I hiss back," Melanie remarked.

"What's going on between you two? You were such good friends," Christina said.

Melanie shook her head. "He's just gotten so competitive. It's like he's always trying to be better than me."

Christina arched one brow. "But *you're* the one always trying to be the best. The best groom, the best exercise rider, the best jockey. Isn't that why you're doing all those exercises and not eating?" she demanded.

"Well, if I'm ever going to make it as a jockey, I have to be all those things," Melanie said in self-defense.

Just then Ashleigh came into the kitchen doorway. "Your dad wants to speak to you again." She gave Melanie a reassuring smile. "It's all right. He's through biting off heads."

Melanie hurried into the family room.

"Melanie, Ashleigh and I agree on your punishment," her father said. "Ashleigh thinks most of the problem was how hard you were working at the farm."

"I have been," Melanie said. "And I really love—"

"I know how important it is to you," her father cut in. "But I also know how important school and friends are. You and Ashleigh are going to work out a contract that balances all the activities in your life. When you have it finalized, I want you to call me and let me know what you've worked out. Does that sound fair?"

Relief flooded through Melanie. "Really fair, Dad. And I promise I'll pull my grades up."

"Great. Because if you don't"—Melanie heard her father's voice harden—"I'm going to tell Ashleigh that you will not be allowed to ride during the week."

Melanie's heart fell to her knees. "Right, Dad," she said flatly. After saying goodbye, she hung up and fell back on the sofa, drained. *Well, the worst didn't happen,* she thought. *Yet.*

Ashleigh came in with a pad of paper and pencil. "Let's do this right now. Earlier you mentioned time management." She held out the paper. "So you decide what you're going to give up in order to make room for school."

"But I can't give up anything!" Melanie protested.

Cocking her head, Ashleigh gave her a stern look. "Don't you want to pull up your grades?"

139

"Yes," Melanie agreed reluctantly.

For the next half hour she wrote, erased, rewrote, and chewed her pencil. Nothing worked. School just took up too much time. And why did everybody insist on time for friends? She had Christina, Naomi, and Samantha right here on the farm. They were all she needed.

After a while Ashleigh came back in. "Well? Any success?"

Reluctantly Melanie handed her the paper. She'd marked it off into seven columns—one column for each day. In each she'd tried to balance school, chores, working out, riding, and everything else.

"You're only planning on half an hour of homework a night?" Ashleigh questioned.

Melanie nodded. "I'm fast."

"Christina!" Ashleigh hollered. A second later Christina came downstairs in her pajamas. "How long does homework usually take you?" Ashleigh asked her daughter.

"At least an hour. Sometimes two."

Ashleigh began to erase, and Melanie rolled her eyes. "That's only because she's slow."

"I am not!" Christina protested.

By the time Ashleigh had finished with the contract, Melanie didn't recognize it. She was relieved to see that she was still Chaser's groom, but dismayed to see that she could work with the horses only until five-thirty on

140

school nights. That wouldn't give her time to do anything at the barn.

"You have me galloping only one horse in the morning," she protested. "And—"

"You can gallop more on Saturdays and Sundays," Ashleigh pointed out. "Except for this weekend."

Melanie glanced up sharply. "What's happening this weekend?"

"You're going on the ride with the others. I should have insisted before."

"Cool!" Christina said.

"But—but—" Melanie's mouth flapped. "But I don't want to!"

"You may not want to, but you need to," Ashleigh explained. "You need to relax and have some fun with your friends before you no longer have any friends. Now sign it, please."

Standing up, Ashleigh handed Melanie the contract. She recognized the determined look in her aunt's eyes and knew she'd better not argue. Exhaling loudly, she signed the contract.

"I'll post this on the refrigerator," Ashleigh said as she went into the kitchen.

Arms folded, Melanie stared gloomily at the family room floor. Okay, so she should be thankful she hadn't been grounded for life. Still, why didn't anyone understand? Why didn't they listen to what she wanted? She definitely did not want to go on the trail ride, especially now that Kevin was going.

"Sorry you're so bummed out," Christina said.

She'd been so quiet, Melanie hadn't realized she was still there.

"It's not your fault," she mumbled.

"And I know you don't want to hear this, but I really do think we'll have a great time this weekend."

Melanie scowled. "You're right. I don't want to hear it." Jumping up from the sofa, she faced her cousin. "I'll go because I have no choice. But don't expect me to be all rah-rah and gung-ho like Katie the cheerleader—because I won't!"

Thursday morning Ian told Melanie to canter Perfection for the first time since his injury. "Slow and easy, and don't let him get away from you," Ian warned.

Melanie nodded. She'd been trotting him every morning around the track, then ponying him every afternoon in the pasture, up and down the hills, until his muscles were hard.

The previous afternoon Dr. Lanum had examined his leg and pronounced him ready for training. Melanie was elated. She really enjoyed working with one horse. Since Stone had left, she'd been bouncing back and forth between different horses. From now on, Ian had promised, she'd be Perfection's rider until he needed a jockey for his first race.

As she rode him to the track, she passed Kevin leaving on Thunder. A fine mist was falling, and the gelding's mane glistened. "I hear you're going on the ride this weekend," he said, halting Thunder.

"Not by choice. I'd rather stay here."

"Mmm. I heard you got in some trouble."

Melanie shrugged. "Nothing I couldn't handle."

They stood awkwardly for a second, the horses pulling on the reins in their eagerness to get moving. Melanie was actually surprised he'd stopped to talk. For the last week they hadn't seen each other except for the bus ride into school, and then Kevin had barely acknowledged her presence even if they sat near each other.

"So how's Chaser the wonder horse doing?" Kevin asked, a hint of sarcasm in his voice.

Melanie didn't like his tone. "Wonderful, as a matter of fact. Sam's ponying him on the track on Saturday." *And I'm going to miss it*, she thought bitterly.

"Sorry I won't be there to witness the miracle horse's first time on the track."

"That's a snotty thing to say," Melanie snapped. "I mean, what is your problem, Kevin? You've had a chip on your shoulder all week. If you're still mad that I'm Chaser's groom, then get over it."

Kevin's brows shot up. "*I've* had a chip on my shoulder? What about you? Ever since you got into this jockey thing, no one's been good enough for you."

"What are you talking about?" Melanie sputtered.

"I'm talking about your attitude," Kevin snapped. "Your I'm-going-to-be-the-next-Derby-winning-jockey-

and-to-heck-with-everyone-else attitude."

"That's not true."

Raising his crop, Kevin pointed it at Melanie. "And for your information, I could care less about being Chaser's groom. T-Bone and I have become a great team. Not that you would have noticed."

Just then Perfection, tired of standing, leaped in the air, almost unseating Melanie. Her feet flew from the stirrups and she flopped onto his neck. Angrily she turned him in a circle, her cheeks burning with embarrassment when she heard Kevin laugh.

When she regained her balance, she thrust her feet into the stirrups and glared at him. "I don't think that was funny."

Kevin's smile died. "That's exactly what I mean. When you first came to Whitebrook, you were really fun to be with. You would have laughed at yourself, too. You've changed, Mel. You just don't realize how much."

"Well, you've changed, too, for your information. You used to be my friend. Now you act like you hate me."

Kevin stared at her a second, then said, "Gee, I'm surprised you noticed how I was acting. I thought you were too busy being the best." Turning Thunder, he rode off.

Melanie was stunned by his words—it was like hearing a harsher version of what Christina had said the other day.

Clucking to Perfection, she steered him through the gap in the railing. The track was damp and his hooves made rhythmic pounding sounds. For a second all Melanie could think about was what Kevin had said. It was true, she had changed. But only because she'd found something she was serious about.

Kevin wasn't totally right. She still enjoyed joking with Christina. It was Kevin who had changed. He'd become solemn and cutting. In fact, being around him all weekend was going to be torture.

"Mel? Are you riding today?" Ian called.

She swung her head around. Ian was waving from the other side of the track. While Melanie was in a daze, Perfection had walked almost halfway around.

"Just warming him up!" Melanie hollered. "He felt a little stiff." She turned him counterclockwise and, squeezing him with her heels, urged him into a trot. Ian had said to canter from the half-mile pole to the finish line only.

When she reached the pole, she crouched lower and kicked him lightly. He broke into a canter that was as smooth as glass.

The wind whistled past Melanie's cheeks, and the fine mist covered her goggles. She dropped them around her neck, then urged Perfection a notch faster.

His stride lengthened, but she could still feel him listening to her, waiting for her signal instead of taking the bit in his teeth and racing off. The hours of grooming, hand walking, and trotting had paid off.

Melanie grinned, letting the thrill take over. Riding a horse as fast and responsive as Perfection made it easy to forget about Kevin and her troubles.

●●●

Saturday morning Melanie slid out of bed before sunrise. At eight o'clock Joe Kisner, one of the weekend workers, was taking Christina, Melanie, Trib, Sterling, and all their supplies to the camp, where they'd meet up with the others. Melanie had packed the night before, so she had plenty of time to work Perfection before she left.

Melanie pulled on her jeans and a sweatshirt and tiptoed down the hall. Ashleigh hadn't said she couldn't ride this morning. She'd just said Melanie had to go to the camp. Melanie had already told Ian she'd ride the colt, so it was on his schedule.

When she heard a noise coming from Mike and Ashleigh's bedroom, Melanie quickened her pace. Hurrying, she dashed through the kitchen to the mudroom. Grabbing a jacket from the hook, she stuck her feet in her boots and clomped outside without lacing them. She wanted to be on Perfection and headed to the track before Ashleigh saw her.

The lights were on in the training barn, casting an orange glow over the stalls. Ian was walking down the aisle with Naomi and Nathan, giving them instructions. Melanie knew that Naomi and her brother were headed over to the racetrack later to jockey. Melanie wished she could go with them.

"Morning," she called as she headed into the tack room to get Perfection's grooming box.

Naomi and Nathan mumbled sleepy hellos. Ian

146

nodded, then continued with his instructions.

As Melanie brushed Perfection she listened for Ashleigh's voice. The only person she heard was Kevin. Surprised, she peered outside the stall. He was headed for Thunder's stall carrying an exercise saddle.

Rats. He'd be riding at the same time she was.

She hurried through Perfection's grooming. The colt felt Melanie's haste. He began to paw, sending up sawdust, until she told him to stop with a yank on the lead line.

Surprised, he threw his head up in the air.

"Sorry," Melanie told Perfection guiltily, rubbing under his mane until he wiggled his lip. "You weren't doing anything wrong." She was going to have to calm down.

Taking the colt out of the stall, she hooked him to the crossties, then saddled and bridled him. From the corner of her eye, she saw Kevin lead Thunder from the barn. She pretended she didn't notice him.

Ian gave her a leg up. "Same as yesterday," he said. "Except back up to the three-quarter pole and canter to the wire."

"Easy canter?"

"Easy," Ian confirmed. "It's going to take a few more weeks to leg him up. Mike doesn't believe in rushing."

Just then Melanie saw Ashleigh come out of the training barn. She stared in Melanie's direction but didn't say anything. Ian walked with her to the oval. When Melanie saw Kevin trotting Thunder, she stiffened. Immediately Perfection broke into an uneasy

147

jig. "That's okay, bud." She stroked his neck. He was really picking up on her bad vibes.

Cool it, Melanie told herself. Naomi galloped past on Faith, and Melanie turned her attention to the pair. They looked great together. The week after the filly's race, she'd been worked lightly. Naomi had given her a physical and mental break by trotting her up and down the hills in one of the pastures. Now they were back galloping on the track, and it looked as if the vacation had been good for Faith. She seemed more focused and less tense. Mike had talked about racing her again in a week or two, depending on how she worked.

By the time Melanie rode Perfection onto the track, he was striding calmly. She could feel the power in his muscles, power that would propel him to speeds up to forty miles an hour.

She trotted him to the three-quarter pole. Turning him to the inside rail, she got him collected and ready to canter. When she squeezed him with her heels, he took off. *Too fast,* Melanie thought as she lurched forward onto his neck. Then she realized why.

Kevin and Thunder were galloping right behind her.

"Watch out, slowpokes!" Kevin shouted. "Get off the inside rail!"

Where had he come from? Startled, Melanie jerked the right rein, and Perfection lurched into the center of the track. Thunder raced up alongside. "Eat my dust," Kevin yelled, his tone joking, but the expression on his face was serious.

Melanie automatically crouched lower. "Oh, yeah?" she wanted to holler right back. Perfection responded instantly, his neck reaching out, his stride lengthening.

For one second the two horses were neck and neck.

"You can beat them," Melanie whispered, urging Perfection on with her voice and body. *You want to beat him. And so do I!*

Excitement coursed through Melanie as they galloped along. But the thought of beating Kevin once and for all was even more exhilarating.

"Go, Perfection, go!" she whispered.

Suddenly she caught herself. What was she doing?

Perfection could reinjure his leg. Was she willing to risk that just to beat Kevin?

Leaning her weight back, she tugged on the reins. "Whoa," she told him. "Whoa." Perfection flicked his ears as if to say, *No way. I want to race.*

But Melanie knew they couldn't. She sat even deeper, tightening her hold, and he slowed to a canter. With a whoop, Kevin and Thunder pulled ahead, racing past the finish line a quarter mile ahead of her.

As they trotted toward the finish line Melanie held her breath, gauging Perfection's stride. Was there a slight bobble in his gait? Had her foolish stunt hurt him?

No, he was cantering evenly. Relieved, she let out her breath. For an instant she'd forgotten that the horse she was riding was more important than winning.

She was just glad she'd realized it in time.

15

"WOW, THIS PLACE IS GREAT!" CHRISTINA EXCLAIMED LATER that morning as Joe steered the truck up a winding dirt road.

Great? Melanie peered out the passenger-side window of the big pickup. All she could see were trees, trees, and more trees. Oh, yes, and an occasional rock.

"Where'd Katie find this place?" Melanie asked.

"She camped here with her Girl Scout troop."

The pickup jounced, and Melanie grabbed the handle. "Are there bears up here?"

"Bobcats and coyotes, too," Joe said.

"Get real." Melanie gave him a skeptical look.

"I'm telling the truth. Send someone you don't like into the latrine first," he suggested.

"That'll be Kevin," Melanie muttered, and Christina elbowed her. A whinny came ringing from the trailer.

"Poor Trib's probably getting bounced to death."

"How about Sterling? She's never been in the mountains before. She's probably going to freak out."

"Maybe she and I can stay back in the cabin and play cards," Melanie said, sighing.

"Oh, don't be so grumpy," Christina scolded. "You'll have a great time."

Melanie knew that was one thing she wasn't going to have.

Joe steered the pickup into a clearing and braked. "Home sweet home," he announced before climbing from the truck.

Sitting forward, Melanie peered out the windshield. This place was definitely not cushy Camp Saddlebrook. This was a bathroom-in-the-woods, no-running-water type of camp.

The three cabins were actually lean-tos with one side open. Melanie could see four wooden planks built into the side walls that must be for their sleeping bags. In the center of the clearing was a ring of rocks that even a city girl like Melanie knew was for the fire.

Christina hadn't moved, either. "Well, this looks, uh . . ."

"Rustic?" Melanie guessed.

Trib bellowed again, and Melanie opened the truck door. "I guess we'd better unload the two horses. Where do you think they're supposed to go?"

"Katie said there were paddocks behind the cabins." Christina climbed out after her. The two girls walked behind the lean-tos and found several enclosed areas.

Just then Mona drove up in her van. She was bringing Katie and Dylan and their horses. Samantha was bringing Tor, Kevin, Parker, and their horses.

When Mona parked, Katie jumped from the cab. "Isn't this the greatest place?" she exclaimed.

"The greatest, Katie," Melanie said, trying not to sound too sarcastic.

An hour later, everything was unloaded. Joe and Mona had made sure the horses were settled in the paddocks, then driven off. Samantha and Tor's van was parked under the trees.

Melanie was in the middle lean-to unpacking a few things. She'd claimed one of the top bunks, and her sleeping bag was already stretched out on the plank.

Dylan poked his head inside. "All the comforts of home," he joked.

"Oh, shut up," Melanie teased back.

"We're heading out for a ride," he said. "Katie says there's a great view from one of the ridges."

"I don't think I can stand the excitement," Melanie said, but Dylan had already left.

Melanie pulled her chaps from her pack and put them on over her jeans. Since the sun was bright, it wasn't too cold, but she stuffed gloves in her jacket pocket just in case.

"We're going to stay behind and fix dinner," Sam said when the group was tacked up and ready to go.

"We expect a gourmet feast when we return from

rounding up the strays," Dylan responded with a wry grin.

"How about hot dogs and baked beans?" Tor asked.

"No filet mignon? That's it. I'm going home," Parker said. He was mounted on Midnight, one of Samantha's quieter horses. His arm was still in a cast, so he held the reins with one hand. He was such a good rider, Melanie knew he wouldn't have any problems.

"Lead the way, Katie," Christina said.

"Riders, ho!" Katie called, and she and Seabreeze headed up the trail, Christina and Dylan following. Melanie noticed that Kevin steered his Anglo-Arab, Jasper, behind Dylan.

That was fine with Melanie. She didn't want to be near him, either.

Melanie and Trib brought up the rear. At first Trib was dismayed that he wasn't next to Sterling, but he soon lagged behind the larger horses. Melanie had to keep urging him into a trot to catch up.

"See what happens when you eat too much?" Melanie said. "And don't exercise?"

At the mention of the word *eat*, her own stomach rumbled. In her haste to work Perfection, she'd skipped breakfast. They'd stopped for fast food on the way, but the sight of a greasy hamburger had sent her stomach reeling. Now it was two o'clock, and she wished she'd at least eaten a roll.

They rode about forty-five minutes up a steep trail. The scenery was beautiful, Melanie had to admit. She'd never seen so many trees in her life, and Katie had pointed out and named several unusual birds.

Then something wet splattered on Melanie's hand. She tilted her head back. The sky above was dark with rolling clouds. Where had they come from? Several raindrops plopped on her face.

"Hey, in case anyone didn't notice, it's raining!" Melanie called.

"Maybe it will blow over as fast as it blew in," Christina called back. "The sky looks clear ahead. I think we should try to make the ridge."

"I agree. We've come this far," Parker hollered. "Who thinks we should go for it?"

"I'm going to have to turn back," Kevin said. "I think Jasper might be lame." Jumping off, he picked up his horse's front hoof. "Looks like a stone bruise—I'd better walk him back," Kevin added with a sigh.

Leading Jasper, Kevin headed down the path. When he passed Melanie, he didn't even glance at her.

"Tell Sam we should be back in an hour," Katie told him before starting off.

For ten minutes they continued to climb the rocky trail. The rain fell in spurts, so they weren't getting too wet, but Melanie didn't like the ominous clouds to the west. She figured it was raining hard somewhere, and any minute the clouds could blow their way.

Finally Katie halted Seabreeze. "There's a bridge over a gorge up ahead," she said, "with a cleared spot on the other side. I remember my troop stopped there and had a snack before heading for the top."

"How far is it to the top?" Christina asked.

"About a hundred yards."

"Let's do it," Dylan said.

Leading the way, Katie led them to the gorge. Melanie's eyes widened when she saw the wooden bridge. It might have been fine for fearless Girl Scouts, but she didn't think there was any way the horses would cross.

"If one horse leads, the rest will follow," Katie said. "Who's got the calmest horse? Melanie?"

"No way!" Trib was sturdy but not stupid.

"Too bad Kevin's not here," Christina said. "Jasper will do anything."

"Then it's probably Dakota or Midnight," Dylan said.

"Midnight does not like the look of that bridge," Parker said.

Melanie inched Trib closer and looked down. The gorge wasn't very deep, but the sides were steep and rocky. Gnarled bushes and roots grew from the crevices.

"Sorry, guys," Katie said. "I remembered the bridge as being wider and stronger."

"It probably looks that way when you're on foot. That gives me an idea." Dylan dismounted. "I'll lead Dakota. He'll follow me, and the rest will follow him."

One by one, the horses went over until only Christina and Melanie were left. "I don't think I can ride Sterling over," Christina said nervously. Dancing around Trib, Sterling was eyeing the bridge as if it were a monster.

"Why don't you lead her?"

"I'm afraid she'll run me over," Christina admitted.

"I know. Dismount and have Dylan pony her over on Dakota," Melanie suggested. "She should follow him."

"That's a good idea."

Melanie waved for Dylan to come back over, and they explained what they wanted him to do. Christina dismounted, looped the reins over Sterling's head, and handed them to Dylan.

"I'll wait on the other side in case she bolts," Christina said. "Mel, you wait on this side in case she comes charging back."

Melanie nodded. Christina jogged across the bridge, then turned and whistled encouragingly to Sterling.

Dylan started over, Sterling's head held close to his thigh. Dakota flicked his ears anxiously, but with Dylan's urging, he stepped onto the bridge.

Sterling followed, her hooves echoing loudly on the wood, and she began to dance nervously. Suddenly a streak of lightning ripped through the sky. Trib jumped, Melanie's heart flew into her throat, and Sterling leaped straight in the air.

She came down with such force on the bridge, a wooden plank cracked and her hoof broke through. In total panic, the mare ripped the lead from Dylan's fingers and charged across the bridge.

Melanie heard a second crack. She screamed as another plank snapped under the horses' weight. Dylan nudged Dakota forward, and the gelding scrambled for traction as the bridge seemed to collapse under him.

Lunging forward, Dakota made it to the other side. The force of his jump sent Dylan flying. He tumbled to the ground, the momentum of his fall carrying him to the edge of the gorge.

As he rolled over the side Christina screamed, then slid down the hill after him, catching the sleeve of his jacket. Parker jumped off Midnight, and the two pulled Dylan back up to level ground.

Dakota had run to Sterling and the two touched noses. Sterling was trembling, and Melanie could see blood on her ankle.

"Is Dylan all right?" she hollered.

Dylan was sitting on the edge of the gorge, rubbing his side where he'd fallen. He nodded, and Melanie took a breath.

Then she turned her attention back to the bridge. The whole middle section of planks had fallen into the gorge. There was no way anyone could cross it. Christina, Katie, Dylan, Parker, and their horses were trapped on the other side.

16

MELANIE SHIVERED. HER JACKET WAS WATERPROOF, BUT THE rain was falling harder and the wind was starting to blow. Another bolt of lightning ripped through the sky, and Trib jumped. Raising his head, he gave a forlorn whinny, calling to his friends on the other side. Melanie could only stare in horror at the broken bridge.

What were they going to do? Dylan and the others could probably climb back through the gorge, but there was no way the horses would be able to navigate the steep, rocky sides.

"Melanie! You've got to get help!" Christina's cry jolted Melanie back to reality.

"You guys can climb out!" Melanie called back. "Leave one person with the horses."

"Can't. Dylan's ankle is twisted. We don't want to leave him or the horses. Get Kevin. He knows another path to the ridge. He can lead us back."

The rain was falling harder, and Melanie could barely hear. Had they said to get Kevin? Twisting in the saddle, Melanie looked down the path behind her. It wound like a snake down the hill into the dark woods. Would she find her way back?

"Hurry!" Katie cried.

She had no choice. "Okay!"

Turning Trib, she headed down the path. His ears flew back and she thought he was going to balk without his friends. But then he broke into a jog as if he knew he was headed home.

Melanie jounced in the saddle. The cold wind whipped through the bare branches and boughs. Rain seeped through the shoulders of her jacket. She was chilled and miserable and scared. She tried to remember how long it had taken to climb the hill to the bridge. An hour?

As the thunder rumbled around them, Trib settled into a nervous walk. His ears flicked back and forth.

"You're doing great, Trib," Melanie praised. "When we get back I'll treat you to a bag of carrots."

Above them, lightning flashed. Melanie couldn't believe she was out in the middle of a forest in a thunderstorm. Her fingers were numb on the reins. Remembering her gloves, she dug in her pocket, pulling out one. She almost cried when she realized the other must have fallen somewhere along the way.

Her fingers were so stiff it took forever to pull the

glove on. Tucking the bare hand in her pocket, she held the rein with the other. Not that she had to steer Trib—he seemed to know where he was going. And even if he took a wrong turn, Melanie wouldn't know. She didn't have a clue where she was.

Fear stabbed Melanie's insides. What if she got lost? She'd never be able to help her friends. Without food or water, they'd all perish in the woods.

A crack of thunder made Melanie jump. Using the glove, she wiped her eyes. The rain was falling so hard, she couldn't see. It was as if they were riding through dense fog.

Melanie had no idea how long they'd been traveling. When Trib clambered up an incline, she panicked. Were they going in circles?

After what seemed like forever, the rain began to taper off. Melanie tried to figure out where they were, but all she could see were trees and a huge boulder that looked like a sleeping elephant.

Trib broke into a jog and Melanie swayed in the saddle. Her brain felt like sand, and her body was numb with cold. Her stomach growled; her eyelids drooped. She was so hungry; so tired. She should have eaten. She shouldn't have gotten up so early. She shouldn't have exercised so hard before she left Whitebrook. How was she supposed to rescue her friends if she didn't have the energy to save herself?

Tears blurred her eyes. She'd never get help in time.

Trib stumbled, throwing Melanie forward. Exhaustion overwhelmed her. Wrapping her arms around Trib's neck, she held on.

"Trib, you've got to get us back to the camp," she whispered, her lips moving against the pony's wet mane. "Please hurry. . . ."

"Melanie, wake up." Someone jostled her roughly.

"Shh." Melanie mumbled.

"Melanie, it's Kevin." A hand patted her cheek.

Melanie jerked upright, but lost her balance and with a cry of surprise fell sideways. Kevin caught her and the two tumbled to the ground.

"What in the world?" Melanie pushed herself away from him, bumping into Trib's leg. Totally confused, she glanced around. She was sitting on soggy leaves in the middle of the woods. "What happened? Where am I?"

Standing up, Kevin put one hand under her arm and helped her to her feet. Her legs were so stiff and unsteady, she had to hold on to him.

"You're on the trail about a mile from camp," Kevin explained. "When the rain stopped, I borrowed Tor's horse to ride back and make sure everyone was okay after the storm. That's when I found Trib coming down the trail, you hanging on like you were hurt. You scared me to death."

"I was so exhausted, I must have fallen asleep," Melanie said.

"Where are the others?" Kevin asked.

With a muffled cry, Melanie clapped a hand over her mouth. "The bridge collapsed." Then she burst out crying, the tears streaming down her cheeks.

"The bridge over the gorge?" Kevin asked, his eyes wide.

"Yes. Everybody is all right, but Dylan hurt his ankle," Melanie sobbed. Suddenly she began to shiver. She was soaked to the skin. Kevin unzipped her jacket, pulled it off, and made her take his.

In shaky gasps, Melanie told him what had happened. "I came back to get you. Katie said you know another way to the ridge and could lead them back."

"I did know two years ago—when I was a Boy Scout." He glanced around the woods in frustration. Melanie sagged against Trib. She'd finally stopped shivering and her body was beginning to thaw.

Turning, Kevin opened a saddlebag and pulled out a thermos. "Here. Drink some hot chocolate. I've got some trail mix, too."

"Thanks." Melanie was never so glad to see food in her life. "This morning I left without eating," she confessed. "And I was up so early . . ." Her voice trailed off. "Oh, Kevin, I've been so stupid. I'm supposed to be getting help and here I am babbling about my problems."

Moving away from the horses, Kevin gazed up the path, a frown on his face. "I wish I could remember where that other trail was."

While Kevin looked around, Melanie poured a cup

of hot chocolate and munched on some trail mix. Slowly her head started to clear and she could feel some of her energy returning.

Finally Kevin snapped his fingers. "I do remember. There was a big boulder where the trail forked off to the left."

Melanie stopped in midchew. "The sleeping elephant!"

"What?"

"A big rock that looks like a sleeping elephant. Trib and I passed it coming down the mountain."

"How far up the trail?"

Melanie shook her head. "I have no idea. Right after that I must have conked out." Turning, she patted Trib. Steam rose from his back. His fur was matted and wet. "If it hadn't been for Trib, I wouldn't have made it."

Kevin took the thermos and put it back in his saddlebag. "I'll ride up ahead and find them. You go back to camp and tell Sam and Tor what happened."

Melanie shook her head. "No way. I'm going with you."

He looked at her over his shoulder. "Sure you and Trib can make it?"

She nodded firmly. "I'm sure. I can munch trail mix while I ride."

They mounted. Melanie's legs felt like jelly and her fingers were stiff on the reins. For a second she was worried about Trib, but when Kevin started up the trail, Trib spun to follow Tor's horse, Gunner.

It didn't take long to reach the boulder. Melanie stopped Trib alongside Gunner. "There's the trail," she said excitedly, pointing to a rough cut in the woods that headed left.

"I remember it now," Kevin said. "It crosses the gorge at a low spot, then follows it up to the bridge. The view isn't as nice, so most groups don't hike it. Come on, we'd better hurry before it starts getting dark."

"Or starts raining again," Melanie muttered, steering Trib behind Gunner as they climbed the rocky path.

"Hey! There's the gorge!" Kevin said about twenty minutes later.

Standing in her stirrups, Melanie spotted a rocky crevice zigzagging through the trees. When they got closer, Trib's ears pricked forward and he eyed it warily.

"Don't worry. There's no bridge," Melanie assured him.

"It looks like the crossing's over there." Kevin pointed to the right. Where the gorge was shallow, a path had been worn down one side and up the other.

Gunner strode confidently across it, Trib scrambling behind. They turned right, and as they climbed higher, Melanie knew they were getting closer to the ridge and her friends.

Suddenly she heard a shout. "Kevin! Melanie! It's about time you guys got here!"

Up ahead, Dylan, Katie, Parker, and Christina were

riding toward them on the trail. They looked wet and bedraggled, but safe.

Melanie waved back, her eyes filling with tears at the sight of her friends.

"Come on, let's find out if they're okay," she told Kevin. Melanie squeezed Trib into a trot, and side by side they trotted up the trail.

"Thanks again for rescuing me," Melanie said later that evening to Kevin. They were back at camp, seated around a crackling fire. Kevin sat beside her on a log, and the two held marshmallows on sticks over the coals. Dinner was over, and Christina and Dylan had gone to check on the horses. Tor and Parker had taken the van down to the ranger station to report that the bridge was out. Katie and Samantha were fixing up their bunks for the night.

Everyone had made it through the accident on the bridge without any major injuries. Sterling had a scratch on her hock, but she seemed to be sound. Samantha had taped Dylan's ankle, and except for some slight swelling, it was okay, too.

That left Melanie and Kevin alone. She decided it was now or never if she was going to patch things up with him.

"After the way I've been acting the last couple of weeks," Melanie continued, "I'm surprised you didn't leave me in the middle of the woods."

"Well, I had to think really hard about saving you," Kevin joked. "I knew once I woke you up, I'd have to listen to your big mouth."

"My big mouth!" Melanie exclaimed. "You're the one who's been so touchy and mean."

When Kevin just stared into the fire, Melanie knew she was right. The riff between them hadn't been all her fault.

"I knew something was wrong," she continued. "I just didn't know what."

"Why didn't you try asking?" he said, sounding bitter.

"I tried to talk to you," Melanie explained. "But all you did was bite my head off."

"You never tried to talk to me," Kevin retorted. "You were too busy running around playing supergroom and ace rider. It was as if your old friends didn't count anymore."

Melanie opened her mouth to argue back, but she knew he was right. That was what she'd realized on the trail. In her zeal to be the best, she had neglected her friends.

Everyone had been telling her that in his or her own way—Kevin, Christina, Katie, even Ashleigh. She just hadn't been listening.

"I'm sorry," she said, choking on the words. "I guess I was caught up in my own thing."

"I'm sorry, too," Kevin mumbled, his gaze on his

burning marshmallow. "For being such a jerk."

"Uh, Kev, if you don't watch it, your marshmallow's going to be one big cinder."

Kevin whipped it from the flames. "Hey, I like them black and crispy." He flashed her a big smile, the first she'd seen in a long time.

"So what was bothering you?" Melanie asked, pulling off her own marshmallow. It was lightly browned and gooey. Perfect. She popped it in her mouth.

He sighed. "A lot of things. Basically, I was mad at my dad."

"I'd like to listen," Melanie said between chews. "Is it too late?"

Kevin gave her an embarrassed grin. "It seems so stupid now. I guess it took a crisis to knock sense into both our heads."

Melanie giggled. "Especially your hard one. Were you mad at your father because he made me Chaser's groom?"

"That was part of it. I felt like he never paid attention to me anymore." He glanced hesitantly at Melanie, as if worried she'd think he was foolish.

She nodded solemnly. "I know that feeling."

"I thought being Chaser's groom would at least get him to notice me," Kevin rushed on. "Mike's always appreciative of the work I do around the farm, but sometimes it seems like my dad only criticizes me. When he didn't even ask me about buying Chaser, I was really mad. It was like my opinion didn't count." Twisting sideways on the log, he looked at Melanie, a hurt look in his eyes, "Do you know that after I made the basketball team, he never once congratulated me?"

"He's been preoccupied," Melanie said. "I think he was more worried about buying Chaser than you knew. He just never let on."

Kevin blew out his breath. "He knew Mom and I didn't approve because he had to use all our savings. It meant I couldn't go to the clinic, which I had asked him about this summer. That seems petty, I know, but basketball means a lot to me, yet all he could think about was what he wanted."

"And you took some of your anger out on me?" Melanie guessed.

He gave her a sheepish grin. "I was pretty mad at you. I mean, you've changed, Mel. When you first came, you were goofy and a lot of fun. Now . . ." He shrugged. "Just like you said, it was as if you didn't have time for your friends anymore. I missed you." Flushing hotly, he stared into the trees.

"You had Heather," Melanie teased.

He burst out laughing. "I knew you were jealous."

"Not!" she shot back, but then she said, "Actually, I was jealous—but not of Heather. I was jealous of how good you were with the horses. You even made exercise riding look easy. All I could think about was beating you in a race."

Kevin grimaced. "Perfection would have beaten Thunder that day."

Melanie glanced at him in surprise. "Really?"

"Yes. Thunder doesn't have the speed, and, well, you're good, Mel. You're learning how to push the right buttons on a horse to make it want to give you everything in a race."

Melanie smiled. "Thanks for saying that. Your opinion means a lot to me. But you know what? I learned that winning isn't as important as friends. Next time we race, I'd rather it end in a dead heat. That way we'd both be winners."

Still smiling, she stuck another marshmallow on her stick. "Friends again?" she asked him.

"Friends."

Just then Christina, Dylan, Katie, and Samantha came back to the fire, chattering excited y about the next morning's ride.

For the first time in weeks, a contented feeling filled Melanie. Sunday, when she got back to Whitebrook, she'd take her contract off the refrigerator and really study it. Ashleigh and her dad were right. She needed to find a better balance in her life.

Not that she'd ever give up her dream of being a jockey, Melanie told herself quickly. And she'd continue to work hard with the horses because she loved it. She was just going to remember that dreams were so much richer when they were shared with people you cared about.

"Where are we riding tomorrow?" Melanie asked Katie when she came over to get a stick.

"We'll try the top of the mountain again," Katie explained. "The view really is awesome."

Christina laughed. "Only this time we're taking the safe lower path."

"Sounds great to me," Kevin said.

"Me too," Melanie said as she handed her cousin the bag of marshmallows. "I wouldn't miss being on the ride with you guys for anything."

Alice Leonhardt has been horse-crazy since she was five years old. Her first pony was a pinto named Ted. When she got older, she joined Pony Club and rode in shows and rallies. Now she just rides her Quarter Horse, April, for fun. The author of more than thirty books for children, she still finds time to take care of two horses, two cats, two dogs, and two children, as well as teach at a community college.

◆◆